DIEN-VEK

AN ASHELON NOVELLA

Books by Carolyn Kay

Dien-Vek

An Ashelon Novella

Carolyn Kay

Ashelon Publishing 2017

DEDICATION

To my parents, Barb and Steve. Without your unwavering support and patience, I wouldn't be who I am today. You filled my life with love, open discourse, science, books, and the freedom to explore my passions. You are two of the most amazing people I know, and I'm very proud to be your daughter.

PS – I blame my warped sense of humor on Dad.

Acknowledgements

First, this book wouldn't even be a thing, if not for the love of my life, Chaz Kemp. Ashelon was his brain-child, and he was gracious enough to allow me to play in his world. Thank you. Second, this book wouldn't be the work it is without my editor, Aimee, and my writer's group; Fiction Foundry Freaky Fridays. John, Klara, Jennifer, Robbie, and Sarah, you all rock, and your input was invaluable. Third, without the guidance of many of my peers in the early stages of my writing endeavors, I wouldn't be the emerging writer I am today. So thank you, Travis, Quincy, Jim, Vivian, Chris, and the rest of my 'tribe.' And last, but never least, thank you to my parents, friends, and family for all of your support and encouragement. I couldn't do this without you.

SELDOVIA
ARSU
FREEDONIA
AZETLAN
AYA
ZORROVIA
N
NW
NE
W
E
SW
SE
S

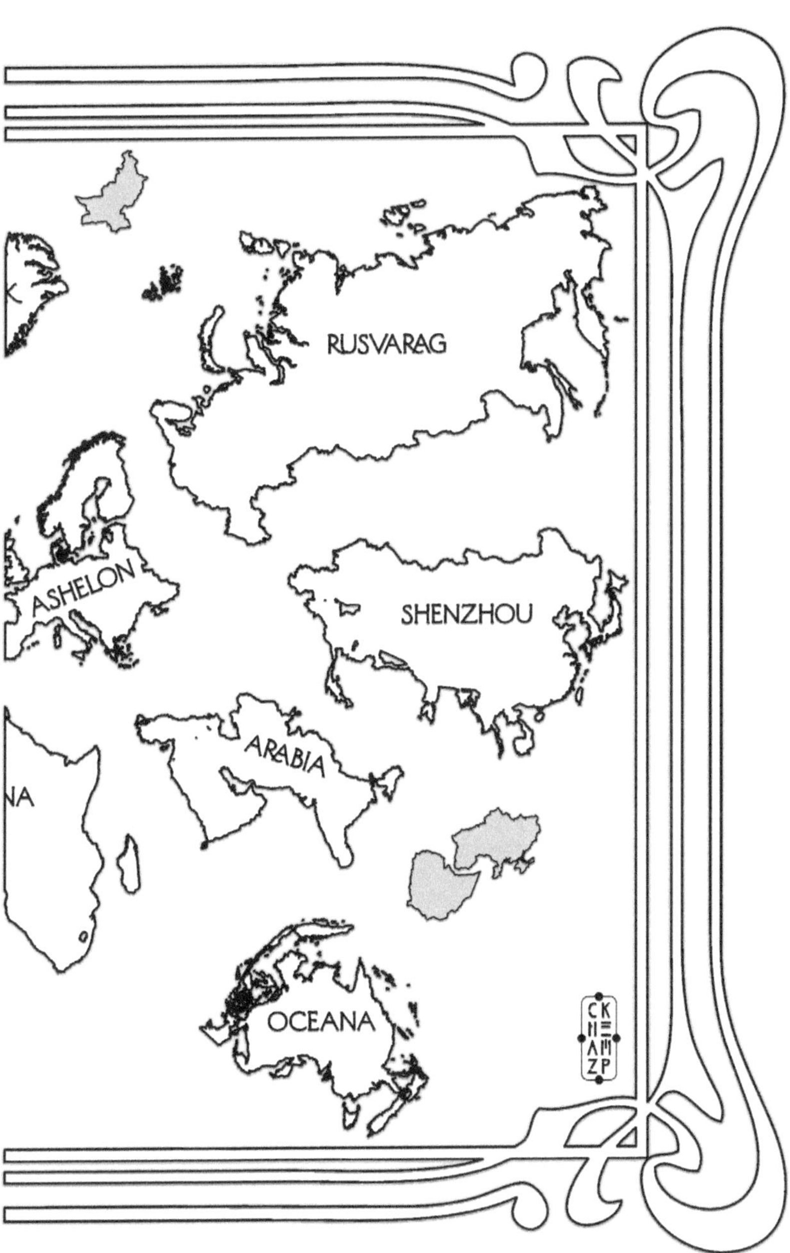

RUSVARAG
ASHELON
SHENZHOU
ARABIA
NA
OCEANA

THE EMPIRE OF
ASHELON
THE YEAR 1850
FOSNA
SVERIGG
LOHJA
SKANE
PRUSSIA
SKOTIA
EIRE
ASHELON
BAVASIA
KIEVKA
GALLIA
SKITAZRA
DEVA
CATALAN
ESPERJA
HELLAS

Chapter 1

Galessel looked over the rail at the clouds passing below, her stomach fluttering. Sunlight passing through the airship's fish-shaped balloon cast purple shadows on the deck. She toyed with one of her ear charms, a small amethyst hung from a thin platinum ring that marked her as a diplomat.

"Worried about your visit to Arturia?" asked the airship's sylph captain, N'hena Nikia.

Galessel started, so focused she hadn't heard the diminutive fae approach. Then she sighed. Apparently she wasn't hiding her nervousness well. Adjusting her goggles, she replied to the airship captain, "A little."

She'd never been to Arturia, Ashelon's capital city, and the prospect of taking her sister's place as ambassador to the human queen filled her with a heady mix of anticipation and dread. A skilled diplomat herself, it wasn't the duties that had Galessel's stomach in knots. It was the idea of walking among mortals without glamour.

The magic all fae used to blend in with mortals had disappeared after a god-sent comet exploded over Zorrovia nearly fifty years ago—an event now called the Great Unveiling. Galessel hadn't been to the mortal realm since. Her duties instead took her across the Hidden Lands in an attempt to calm the various races of the fae in the face of an uncertain future. Humanity could now see them for what they were. Nothing would ever be the same.

"Are you at least enjoying the trip, ambassador?" N'hena asked.

"Delightful as always, captain. Of all of the airships that serve the Hidden Lands, I most look forward to those trips when I book passage on the *Intrepid*."

She caught a pleased pink shimmer pass along the captain's diaphanous wings. Galessel felt like she towered over N'hena, but she was of average height for an elf—as tall as most humans. In her experience, sylph didn't mind the height difference, finding superiority in their ability to fly. And if anyone ever thought N'hena's diminutive stature meant she was a sweet and passive creature, a closer look would make them think twice. The sylph boasted a fearsome array of weapons on her person; her prize twin pistols strapped to her hips, a wicked long knife handle protruded above her head from a sheath on her back, and small knives were secreted in the leather bracers on her wrists.

"I'm honored to have you aboard, even if the destination has you feeling wary," N'hena said.

"Quite. I have never met the Queen of Ashelon, and I'm being asked to negotiate for our people at a critical juncture." Galessel put her hand back on the deck rail, her motion deliberate. "My sister spent weeks with me, going over every detail. She says I'll do just fine, but I still wish the lateness of her pregnancy wasn't preventing her from finishing this."

N'hena set her hand on Galessel's elbow. "I've heard stories of the time you talked down an angry troll at the Crossroads Bridge. Surely talking to a group of humans will be easier."

The purple-haired sylph had a point. It was just a trade negotiation. She'd been in more tense situations by far. "You're right, of course. It should be a simple negotiation. The queen's minister of trade is asking my people to expand our coffee exports. He's gone so far as to demand we triple them. I'm afraid we cannot agree to that." She toyed with her thick ebony braid for a moment before continuing. "And, if you will believe this, he had the audacity to ask for five hundred tons of wood suitable for ship building!"

N'hena narrowed her eyes, her wings changing to an angry red, and waited for Galessel to continue.

"This puts truth to the rumors that the queen wants to expand her air and sea fleets, but with so much of the forests in the mortal realm cut down for firewood by the low-borns, there is no wood for building."

"And what does Ashelon offer in return?" N'hena's wings faded slightly, but stayed red. Her hands strayed to her pistol-grips.

"Gold and chocolate, and Ashelon's good will." Galessel turned back to the rail, her fingers playing with her thick braid.

"That's not much, considering what they're asking for." N'hena shook her head. "The human queen has gotten bold with the backing of her new god."

"Aye, that she has. While the comet diminished our magic in the mortal realm, it strengthened the humans'. Queen Victoria aches to regain the lands she lost when the natives used their magic to rebel." Galessel sighed. "At least the Hidden Lands are safe."

"For now. Although she could sure use our resources to gain back Freedonia and Aryadi." N'hena's wings turned yellow at the thought. "Damn the comet and Asher to the Dark!" Red pulsed through her wings, making them shimmer like fire, as she cursed the god of chaos. "Victoria continues to spread strife and chaos throughout the mortal realm, which only serves to make Asher more powerful. I wish I knew how he convinced her to become his high priestess."

Galessel shrugged. "Power? Humans seem obsessed with it."

The *Intrepid's* first mate, a brute of a man—Galessel suspected he was actually part giant—thumped toward them, stopping in front of N'hena.

"Cap'n, there's a ship to starboard. It's not approaching, but I think you should come have a look."

N'hena nodded, her wings transitioning to a pale, creamy yellow. "If you'll excuse me, Princess." She tugged on her leather vest and looked behind Galessel to the large, twin elven guards standing a discreet distance away. "You might want to return to your cabin. I'm sure it's nothing, but better to be safe."

A chill ran over Galessel, causing her to clutch her shawl around her more closely. "Of course, captain."

N'hena bowed, then motioned for her first mate to lead the way. His long legs took him down the deck quickly. As her wings came up to speed, the small sylph lifted from the deck and flew after him, catching up within moments.

Turning to her guards, Galessel found them watching the captain's progress. Rare for elves, they were identical twins, but she could tell them apart easily. Daylor, the older of the two, kept his facial hair trimmed to a crisp mustache and goatee, while his brother preferred modest mutton chops. "Daylor, follow the captain and find out what's of concern."

"Yes, m'lady." Daylor looked pointedly at his brother Garrik, who nodded.

"We should take the captain's advice, m'lady," Garrik said, pointing the way down the port side to her cabin as Daylor walked briskly, his armor chiming, in the opposite direction.

Curious, but not willing to fight her guards, she headed to her cabin.

⊛ ⊛ ⊛

"... black ship ... maybe pirates ... Svellvega."

That last, the name of her people's long-time enemy, snapped Galessel fully awake. Her book lay open on the same page she'd opened it to earlier. She must have dozed off. Looking up, she found her guards whispering in the far corner of her cabin. Both now held their silver helms under an arm. What was going on?

"Was I dreaming? I thought I heard you say something about the Svellvega?"

Both elves turned to her, their faces concerned. "It's nothing m'lady. Just idle speculation," Daylor said.

Galessel pushed herself into a more comfortable sitting position on the bed and rubbed at a sore spot in her neck. "There's nothing idle about the Svellvega, Daylor. What did you see?"

"Nothing specific, m'lady. Just another airship,

several leagues distant, but paralleling our course. We lost it in the clouds before anyone could discern its flag," Daylor said, running his free hand through his curly blonde hair.

Daylor had been her guard since she was forty—more than thirty years. She could tell he was holding something back. Annoyance and concern were beginning to make her stomach sour. "Out with it, Daylor. What aren't you telling me?"

Daylor looked at his twin, Garrik, who just shrugged. Galessel slammed her book shut. Daylor had the good sense to look chastised. "It may be nothing, Your Highness. The clouds were creating shadows—"

"And?"

"The ship may have been black."

Black? A chill ran along Galessel's arms. Reports of raids on villages at the far edges of the Hidden Lands often contained descriptions of black airships. The raids only ever left one or two survivors, whose sole purpose was to tell others who was responsible: the Svellvega. "How far are we from Arturia?"

"We'll be there in a few hours." Daylor looked at her, shrugging a single shoulder. "I'm sure it was nothing to be concerned about, Princess."

The Svellvega had never been reported this close to a large human city. Maybe the shadows were playing tricks. That rationale did little to calm Galessel's stomach, but it was the most logical explanation, and it would have to do.

"I'm sure not, but regardless, I have no doubt that N'hena will keep her crew on high alert until we land." The room suddenly seemed claustrophobic with the two large guards taking up one wall. "I think I'll try to take a proper nap, so I'm refreshed when we land. Why don't you two help keep watch outside?"

Both elves seemed more than happy to comply and left without a word. Setting her book on the bedside table, Galessel laid down, but sleep eluded her.

intrepid

Chapter 2

Galessel smoothed out her pale green silk gown and checked her image in the mirror to make sure her braid was tidy and her ear charms were hanging straight. She ran a finger up the edge of her right ear. A silver hoop for gaining the rank of scholar; silver ring and opal bead for Services to Those in Need; obsidian, emerald, and sapphire rings marking her as the chosen liaison to the fire fae, lake sprites, and ravela, respectively.

Her finger lingered on her newest charm. Though she'd had an earring denoting her status as an ambassador for nearly twenty years, she'd just changed out the plain gold ring for one with an amethyst jewel suspended from it, marking her as an ambassador to the human realm. Her pride swelled, before quickly getting quenched by nervous acid. She'd only been to the human realm a few times, and never as the representative of her people. Her sister, Miniel, had assured her that the nobles and the queen would recognize in her charms the nobility and status she held, but she wondered still.

The youngest of three girls, Galessel would never sit on the Anisbarii throne, and thus would never have a platinum ring in her left ear tip. The only time the rings on her left ear would change would be when she married and gained a gold ring with gems in the colors of her house and that of her husband.

A polite cough behind her snapped her out of her thoughts.

"Your Highness? We're about to land," Garrik's bass voice announced from the cabin's doorway.

Embarrassed at being caught mirror-gazing, Galessel turned, keeping her hot cheeks from Garrik's eyes. "Thank you, Garrik. I'll be along shortly." She knew without looking that he bowed to her before leaving, his soft boots whispering against the deck planks as he retreated a few steps down the hall.

Anticipation fluttered in her stomach. Her friend Clove had told her stories of Ashelon, and her sister had briefed her, of course, but they offered vastly different views of the city. Miniel talked mostly of court intrigue and the who's who of the nobility. She knew who was having affairs with whom, and what subplots were important to the Hidden Lands' interests.

Clove's tales, by contrast, were gritty and often dark. Her official occupation was as messenger between the courts of Ashelon and the Hidden Lands, but she also used her access to report on dealings Miniel would never see as a princess and ambassador. Galessel knew the true nature of the city would lie somewhere in between, but wondered if she'd actually see it, or just the pageantry of the court. With Clove as her official guide during her stay, she hoped they'd be able to sneak off to visit with the commoners. Reports on the condition of many fae living in Ashelon was troubling. Her parents didn't appear to be concerned, but Clove confided during her last visit to court that human-fae interactions were becoming increasingly volatile.

The floor beneath Galessel tipped, causing her to step backward and collide with the bed, on which she sat down rather ungracefully. She stayed on the bed until the ship leveled out with a second, more gentle bump. As if the sudden commotion outside her cabin hadn't indicated that they'd landed, the knock on her door from Garrik seemed redundant.

"Coming!" she sang before he could say anything. Grabbing her cloak off the back of the chair, she joined her guards in the hall.

⚕ ⚕ ⚕

Walking out on the deck, Galessel immediately noted the grey pall that hung over the landing platform. The sun was a sickly orange spot in the sky above. She took a deep breath, hoping to rid her lungs of the stale cabin air, and immediately regretted it as she started coughing. The air tasted like charcoal and smelled worse than the fire-fields of the salamander kin. How could the humans stand to breathe? N'hena appeared at her elbow, a scented kerchief in her outstretched hand.

"Here, this will help until you get used to it, Your Highness."

"Get used to it? Is that even possible?" Galessel accepted the kerchief and held it to her nose. Lavender and rose filled her nose.

"So Clove tells me, but I always make an effort to spend as little time on the ground as possible, so I wouldn't actually know." N'hena shook her head when Galessel offered the kerchief back to her. "No, you keep it, Highness. I have others. If you'll excuse me, I should see to the unloading of our cargo." She bowed, her wings blushing a rosy hue. "It was a pleasure to have you aboard, Princess. I will see you in a few days."

"I look forward to it, captain. Thank you."

⚙ ⚙ ⚙

The Anisbarii house carriage was waiting for them in the lot at the airfield. In an attempt to fit in better with the humans, her parents had commissioned a carriage with a mechanical horse when they bought the townhome residence within the noble's district. Unlike a typical horse-drawn carriage that required anywhere from two to four horses, the Anisbarii carriage had only the front half of a single mechanical horse attached to what appeared to be a normal four-wheeled black carriage.

The driver steered the gear and steam workhorse via levers instead of reins and the hydronium-powered steam compartment was cleverly hidden under the driver's box.

One of the first to adopt such a conveyance, the Anisbarii were hailed as patrons of the sciences. Galessel, while understanding and supporting her parents' reasoning behind its commission, couldn't stand the mechanical half-horse. The glow in its eyes put her in mind of an agar roch—the feared blood unicorn— and she avoided looking at the beautifully detailed yet unnatural thing as she neared the carriage and the blonde faun standing beside it.

Galessel's small, deer-like friend loved defying fashion trends, preferring to mix and match her wardrobe as if she pulled items from a circus trunk every morning. Her bright red peasant blouse was topped with a riotous-colored patchwork vest. A bright blue sash wrapped around the top of black and white striped bloomers with a ruffle of yellow lace at the knee, and royal purple spats covered her mechanical prosthetic hooves, hiding their unnatural nature.

Galessel embraced her best friend. "Oh, Clove! It's so good to see you."

"And you my friend." Clove stepped back to take in her friend, the pistons in her prosthetic ankles hissing softly. "I'm glad your mother asked you to replace Miniel."

Galessel nodded as she sniffed from the scented handkerchief again. "I'm honored at the opportunity, but I've been away from the mortal realm for so long, I'm worried they've changed since I was here last." It didn't help to quash her worries that what she'd heard of the human queen, Victoria, wasn't very favorable.

Clove smiled, the wind from the propellers of the *Intrepid* causing her garish patchwork vest to flap like a panicked bird against her scarlet blouse. Galessel admired her friend's complete disregard of fashion trends on either side of the veil. She, herself, didn't have that kind of freedom.

With a glance at a pocket watch tucked into a small pocket in her vest, Clove grabbed Galessel's hand and pulled her toward the carriage. "Come on. We should get going before the evening work bells ring. The streets become nearly impassible once the workers are let go for the night."

As her guards took their posts in the carriage box, Galessel climbed inside the carriage with Clove. Puffs of lavender engulfed them, as they found their seats on the padded cushions.

As they traveled through the city, Galessel steeled herself against the noise and the smell. The scented cushions did little to mask the smell of excrement and coal fires. Coal dust settled on their clothes and left smudges on the door frame of the carriage. Galessel looked out the small window as they passed through the suburbs of Arturia. Coal powered buggies and horse-drawn carriages far outnumbered hydronium-powered conveyances. The closer they traveled into the city center, the more foot traffic increased, and their speed noticeably reduced.

"How is it that the humans are still using coal?" Galessel asked her friend. "Hydronium is so much cleaner."

Clove laughed. "You really have been gone from the mortal realms for too long, Galey," she replied. "Hydronium's only accessible to the rich here. The humans have to trade with the dwarves, just like we do, but it's harder to transport in large enough quantities to meet the demand of the masses."

Galessel thought about that for a moment. "I suppose

I take for granted the fact that magic is not as powerful here as it is in the Hidden Lands. Do they not employ the services of a water elemental to keep the moisture from the crystals during transport?"

"Aye, some do, but the elementals' prices are high, so it adds to the cost of the hydronium." Clove's ears rotated back in agitation and her tone became serious. "Of course, there are some who have enslaved the elementals. If you find cheap hydronium, it's a good bet that they deal with an elemental slaver."

"There must be laws against that here. That's abhorrent!" Galessel had heard rumors, but hadn't believed them. No one could be that cruel.

"Parliament tried to pass a series of laws guaranteeing fae and elemental rights last year, but my sources say high-ranking business interests convinced enough members to vote against it." Clove's ears drooped. "There are groups rallying for fae rights, but there are just as many rallying against them. We haven't made much progress in fifty years, I'm afraid."

Galessel saw Clove's ears twitch a scant half second before a commotion erupted outside the carriage, and they lurched to a halt. Both women peeked out the window, faces half hidden by the curtains as the guards jumped down from their perches to stand protectively in front of the carriage door. They could hear raised voices outside, but saw nothing thanks to the bulk of the elven guards.

"By the goddess, move, Garrik!" Galessel grumbled, more to vent her frustration than to actually voice a command. She knew better than to countermand her guards in a strange city. She looked to Clove, whose ear was pressed to the side of the carriage, her eyes closed in concentration. "What do you hear?"

"There's a crowd outside demanding to speak with you, Galey. They recognize the house seal and the horse. They know one of the royals is in here."

"Are they fae?"

Clove shrugged. "I think so. Not many humans would know the house seal."

Galessel began knocking on the door. "Then I have to talk to them." These were her people. Of course she would speak to them. "Open the door, Garrik!" she yelled this time.

The door cracked open, Garrick stood directly in the opening. "I'm sorry, Your Highness, we can't let you out. There's a mob out here."

"But it's a fae mob, yes?"

Garrik nodded. "For your safety, Princess, please stay inside."

Galessel pushed on the door. "I have faith that you can protect me. I'll stay right here. Put down the step so that I may see above them. If something happens, I can duck inside quick as a pixie."

With a heavy sigh, Garrik nodded, turning to whisper something to Daylor. Within moments, the step had been lowered, and the guards pushed the crowd back enough for Galessel to open the door and step out.

The smell of the unwashed mass of people and the refuse in the street nearly made her gag. The crowd standing before her and surrounding the carriage was mostly fae: a mix of trolls, gnomes, lower elves, and a few sylph, but there was also an occasional human in the group. All were dirty, tired, dressed in ragged clothes, and so very angry.

She couldn't understand anything the crowd was yelling. She raised her hands in a gesture asking for silence. They continued to yell until a gnome cobbler stepped forward, a pair of unfinished shoes with their laces tied together over his shoulder. The crowd quieted down.

He bowed, but not very deeply, before speaking. "Your Highness, forgive us for impeding your travel, but we felt there was no other way. Our pleas to your parents have gone unheard, and things are getting worse here."

Pleas? She'd heard nothing of this at court. She looked down, into the dark of the carriage. Clove shook her head, miming not to say anything. "My dear cobbler, gentle fae, due to my lengthy time away from the mortal realms, I am unaware of your situation. Please tell me what wrongs have been done." She heard Clove groan, and hint of lavender wafted up to her as the faun sat down heavily, mumbling something about "here we go."

The crowd all started talking at once, a cacophony of voices that hurt the ears. Her guards closed in around her.

"Stop!"

The crowd's eyes glowed silver as her intent flowed over the crowd. "Quiet down. I can't understand you if you all talk at once."

The crowd immediately quit talking. Some looked like they wanted to continue speaking, but couldn't—as if their voices didn't work.

"Mr. Cobbler, if you would, tell me your name and what is happening to our people."

The gnome stepped forward again. His eyes no longer glowed."I'm called Leatherfoot, Your Highness." He clutched a shoe tightly in his hand, his thumbs worrying the sole as he looked around the crowd. "Not to be disrespectful in any way, Your Majesty, but maybe it would be better if we could meet somewhere quieter? The list of wrongs is long, and we should all be away before the curfew bell rings."

Curfew bell? Miniel hadn't mentioned a curfew. Galessel hadn't heard of one in Arturia since the days of the Great Faerie Riot less than a decade after the Great Unveiling. This did not bode well. "Very well, Mr. Leatherfoot. Do you have a shop?" He nodded, still worrying the sole of the shoe hanging from his shoulder. "Then I shall call there on the morrow, a few hours before noon."

"I—I'd be honored, Your Highness." He bowed deeply.

"Good, be so kind as to give my men the location of your shop." Addressing the crowd, she said, "Please, good people. Go to your homes. I would not be the cause of any trouble. Rest assured that I will hear of your troubles tomorrow." She willed them all to disperse quietly. Their eyes flashed silver in response."Now, go in peace." As the crowd quietly left, almost fading into the evening shadows, she caught sight of a flash of gold in a pointed ear. It couldn't be. She looked back over her shoulder, looking for the unlikely, before ducking back into the carriage. The door closed smartly behind her.

A rap on the top of the carriage started them forward again, and Galessel settled in her seat, fidgeting to get the cushions to release some of their lavender scent. Even with the door closed, she couldn't get the stench of the street out of her nose. But that was a minor annoyance compared to what she may have just seen.

"What's the matter, Galey?" Clove was staring at her with an odd look.

"Huh? Sorry. I thought I saw something—someone— in the crowd as it was dispersing, but I had to have been mistaken."

"Judging by the look on your face it wasn't an old friend. Who did you see that has you so concerned?"

"I didn't see a face, just an ear. A pointed one with a gold ring in the top."

Clove sat back in her seat, her ears flat against her head. "You think you saw a Svellvega?"

"It might have been a trick of the light, a shadow."

Galessel tried to convince herself she had been mistaken and failed. Her hand strayed to her own ear tip, running along the edge and the rings piercing it.

"I haven't seen any reports that the Svellvega are raiding in the mortal realms, but that doesn't preclude their use of spies here." Clove tugged on an ear, deep in thought. "You don't think they noticed you used your gift just now, do you?"

"It depends on how long they were there. It's hard to miss when my eyes, or those I affect, glow. If they missed it, then my secret may be safe. Knowledge of my silver tongue is limited outside my family. Let's hope they don't know it can be passed down."

"Your grandmother's gift was fairly common knowledge. It wouldn't take much to put the pieces together." Clove looked her in the eyes. "You need to be more careful, Galey. If the queen finds out you can influence people at will, she'll ban you from court."

Galessel ducked her head, cutting off eye contact. It was rare for her to use her gift. Learning to control it had taken nearly a decade of grueling, painful lessons. She hadn't spared a thought about using it today, and that scared her.

"You're right, of course. To be honest, I didn't even think about it. I've been gone from the mortal realm for too long. I've forgotten how much more wary I need to be here."

"About that," Clove leaned forward, resting her elbows on her thighs. The added pressure made her ankles hiss. "Galey, I'm not sure it's wise to meet the cobbler at his shop. It's not exactly in a good part of town. And with all the unrest lately, you're likely to get mobbed again."

"Then you'll just have to fill me in on what's been going on, so we can plan for whatever may happen."

galessel

Chapter 3

The next morning Clove found Galessel reading the previous night's *Ashelon Independent* while sipping coffee at the dining table. A plate of scones sat untouched nearby.

"So, what do you think, Galey?" Clove asked in reference to the paper, as she grabbed a scone.

Galessel set her cup down and folded the paper neatly before answering. "I will be surprised if the queen lets them stay in business for long. They are not shy about printing stories that paint her in an unflattering light." She pointed to a story visible on the front page.

"Here they're going on about new laws she's pushed the parliament to pass, giving her sovereignty over lands held by the East Aryadi Company to 'better protect the friends of the Empire,' and how some believe it's a thinly veiled land grab for the empire and has more to do with protecting profits than people."

Clove nodded and swallowed a bit of scone before commenting. "Aye. Word on the street is that it's not just lands held by the East Aryadi Company that she's after."

The fact that Clove did not elaborate made Galessel suspicious, and she looked pointedly at her friend. "Out with it, Clove. What have your sources told you? "

"It's just rumors now, love, but some say she's after the Hidden Lands, too."

"What? She wouldn't dare!" Galessel stood and began pacing. "Have my parents heard of these rumors?"

"Aye. They dismissed them as idle rumors."

Galessel stopped her pacing and faced her longtime friend. "And you didn't see fit to tell me before now?"

Clove shrugged and took another bite of scone, covering her mouth while talking around it. "We were distracted yesterday. Besides, it's merely rumors right now, and there's no hard evidence that she'd be that stupid."

Galessel sat down with a thump, her face somewhat pale. "Oh, I believe she would do just that. With the backing of a god, what's to stop her from finding the gates and blowing right through them with some magic spell gifted her by her most divine patron?"

A servant entered to tell them the carriage was waiting out front to take them to the cobbler's.

"I still don't think this is a good idea, Galey." Clove finished the last of her scone, wiping the crumbs on a napkin.

"We're bringing extra guards." Galessel gently set her teacup down. "These are our people, Clove. I know they're unhappy, but they won't riot just because I pay a visit."

"You don't know how bad things are here. Rumors have been flying that the fae are responsible for the food shortages and the Crown has been targeting fae businesses, shutting them down with false accusations of illegal activities." Clove laid her ears back. "Relations between us and the humans is almost as bad as it was after the Great Unveiling."

"Then that's all the more reason for me to go. I have an audience with the queen tomorrow, and I'd like to know as much as possible about the situation before I go." Galessel stood, smoothing out her green floral day dress. The boning on the corset constricted her movement and more importantly, her breathing, but her sister insisted that she dress as those in Ashelon did. "Come, we wouldn't want to be late."

⊛　⊛　⊛

The buildings in the market district closed in on the carriage like trolls frozen in the sun. Galessel shivered as they passed through the shadows, and Clove's ears twitched constantly.

Galessel's guards closed in around her and Clove as they exited the carriage. They formed a wall of blue and silver lacquered armor that was impossible to see around, and they started moving down the street, the two women enclosed within their ranks.

Clove poked at the one directly in front of her, earning her a backward, scowling glance. "Unless one of you knows the way to the cobbler's from here, you're going to have to let us see where we're going." She stomped a hoof in annoyance, the clear tone of metal on stone echoed off the close-knit buildings. The guards didn't part.

"Do I have to order you to do as she says, or can we just get on with this?"

Galessel put a reassuring hand on Garrik's arm as he and another guard separated, making room for her and Clove to walk between them. She knew better than to walk before them, and let Clove take a two step lead in front of her. "Thank you," Galessel said quietly. A very slight nod was Garrik's only response.

They walked down the narrow, dirty street in silence. The ring of Clove's metal hooves and the guards' armor, rustling like wind chimes, brought heads peeking out from dim windows and around corners. Despondent beggars looked up from empty bowls as they walked by. A few smiled. Some rattled their bowls, and a few spat on the ground at their passing. All were fae. Galessel's heart broke. Her people, brought so low. She'd been told that things were bad for many fae in the human cities, but she hadn't been able to comprehend the depths of their sorrow until now. She made a mental note to send someone from the townhouse back with as much money and food as they could to distribute to those in need here. There were times like this after the Great Unveiling, but it had gotten better in the intervening years. What had happened to set things back? She hoped Leatherfoot would have some answers.

As they walked, they gathered a following, not only of fae, but of humans, as well. Shopkeepers sent their children to follow or closed up shop to join the procession. Galessel's guards began to close ranks, stepping up to walk evenly with Clove, who gave them barely a glance as she strode down the street.

Leatherfoot was waiting nervously outside his little shop, as they rounded the corner into the market proper. He stood there, his eyes constantly moving, his thumb buffing a circle on the sole of a half-finished shoe, dressed in what was probably his least threadbare set of clothes. He bowed low as the elven party approached.

"Go home, you pompous elf! We don't need more of your kind 'ere!" Someone yelled from a second story window nearby. The cry was taken up by others behind them.

"Please, Your Highness, come inside. No one will bother us." Leatherfoot gestured inside the shop, looking like he didn't believe himself.

Garrik nodded toward the shop. "Lanion, you and Rosmer go inside with the princess. The rest of us will take up positions out here."

Galessel and Clove followed the visibly shaking Leatherfoot inside his shop, the two guards close on their heels.

It took her eyes a moment to adjust to the dim interior. The shop's large front windows were boarded up, the frames bare of any glass. A large rack of candles lit a corner of the shop, where Leatherfoot's work table sat. Tools were neatly arranged, and the mate to the shoe he was currently using for a worry-stone sat next to a roll of leather. Several gnome-sized chairs surrounded a smaller table in the opposite corner near the fireplace, while two larger chairs Galessel assumed for either human or larger fae customers—sat near the boarded windows. Several shelves of finished shoes of all sizes and types lined the wall near the work table. Leatherfoot ushered them toward the larger chairs, and a plump female gnome brought two smaller chairs to join them.

"Your Highness? Miss?" Leatherfoot started. His cheeks flushed pink in embarrassment.

"Just call me Clove, Mr. Leatherfoot," Clove said with a smile.

"Ah, my apologies, Miss Clove. And, it's just 'Leatherfoot.'" He took the hand of the other gnome, bringing her forward. She kept her eyes down, her hands knotted in her apron. "This is my wife, Thistle."

"You honor us, Thistle, Mr. Leatherfoot, by inviting us into your home and business," Galessel replied.

Poor Thistle looked like she was about to faint. Leatherfoot patted her hand. "My dearest, would you be so kind as to fetch us all something to drink, and that wonderful cake you made earlier?"

The request snapped Thistle out of her shyness. "Oh my! Where are my manners? Of course. Please excuse me." She ran off toward the back of the dwelling, after dropping a hasty curtsey.

"Please, Your Highness, Clove, sit. I'm sorry I cannot offer you better accommodations."

"I am not one for velvet cushions and overstuffed pillows, Mr. Leatherfoot. This is just fine," Galessel said as she sat down. Truth be told, she couldn't really tell how padded the seat was due to her damnable bustle. She tried not to fidget overmuch as she found a mostly comfortable position. "Please, tell us of what's happened here. There are so many fae begging in the streets, and your shop looks to have seen better days. If you'll forgive my bluntness."

Leatherfoot focused on his shoe, his thumb making circles on the sole. "I was a babe when the comet hit. I grew up during the worst years of the Hammer Guardians' terror against the fae. My parents almost returned to the Hidden Lands when your mother called us all home. But they decided to stay here, determined to keep the cobbler shop open, to do what they could to show the humans we were not worthy of their hate and fear." He looked up, a slight smile on his face. "Things eventually got better. My father built a successful business. He even made shoes for the queen, shortly after she gained the crown. I took over that business, and it grew even more. I had a large shop in the West End, with well-to-do clients of many folk." His hands tightened on the shoe, knuckles turning white. "And then the eviction notice came. I had two days to vacate my shop, which I'd purchased, or I'd be thrown out."

Clove exhaled sharply through her nose, an indication of anger Galessel knew all too well, but her friend stayed silent.

"I was to be given a small shop—this one—in recompense. But no reason was given."

Thistle appeared, her hands full with a tray of lemon cake and a pitcher of lavender tea. "We, of course, refused." Thistle took up the story when Leatherfoot excused himself to grab a low table for his wife. "Two days later, on the nose, the city guard shows up and throws us out. Piled everything we owned in the street, then mocked us while we struggled to get it all in a cart."

Leatherfoot appeared with the table and took the tray from his wife, setting it down gently. He took Thistle's hand as they both sat. She dabbed her eyes with a kerchief. "They surrounded us, and pushed us at gunpoint all the way here." She sniffed, looking sadly at her husband, who patted her hand.

"We weren't the only fae who were evicted that summer. Every shop owner who was fae or suspected of being sympathetic or friendly to us was forced out."

Galessel held up a hand and turned to Clove. "Why did we not hear about this?"

Clove's ears drooped. "Your parents did. I told them myself, Galey. They claimed there was nothing they could do. Queen Victoria was becoming contentious and they didn't want to escalate tensions. That was also the summer the Svellvega began raiding again."

It was Galessel's turn to huff. "That's still no excuse."

Leatherfoot leaned forward. "Your mother and father did offer to help. They sent us supplies, even offered to bring us back to the Hidden Lands, but we declined. He looked at his wife, his eyes softening. "We'd built our lives here. Our children's friends were all here. We couldn't uproot them."

Thistle nodded, pouring out tea into chipped cups and handing them around with a slice of cake. It all smelled divine, but Galessel's stomach was sour from Leatherfoot's tale.

"While things were never very good after that, we got by. We were happy. I made shoes for the folk here, and everyone got along. And then, about six months ago, it started getting worse again. The human merchants who traded in hydronium stopped coming by, and the price of food and other goods started climbing. No one knows why. Human gangs have started harassing the fae folk again. Comments like you heard earlier are common now if we go to market. Some of the humans here will still trade with us and buy our goods, but most avoid us now for fear of bringing violence upon themselves."

"Hooligans broke our windows. We replaced them at great expense, and the very next week they were broken again. We couldn't afford to fix them, and now most folks think the shop is closed. I'm not sure how we'll get through this winter." Thistle blinked back more tears. She picked at her cake for a moment before setting it aside. No one had an appetite.

Galessel set her tea aside, as well. Anger and the corset made it hard to breathe. She blinked back tears. How could her parents let this happen? The treaties clearly outlined that discrimination by either side would be discouraged and dealt with promptly, but if the Ashelon crown was behind this, it would take more than just a few coins and some supplies to make things better.

"I haven't been to the mortal realms for many years, and I am unknown at court here, but I will get to the bottom of this." Galessel stood, unable to sit any longer. The others followed suit. "I cannot make any promises, but you have my word that I will do everything in my power to see that things are made right."

Thistle took Galessel's hands in hers, her eyes slick with tears. "May the Goddess bless you, Your Highness, and guide you."

The clash of wind chimes preceded another of Galessel's guards, as he ran in from the back of the shop. "We have to leave now, Your Highness. A mob approaches."

"Go out the back—through the alley. It dead-ends into a brick wall. Press the blue brick. It will open a path back to your carriage." Leatherfoot ushered them to the back as voices began to rise outside.

"Rosmer, take the princess, move as fast as you're able. I'll bring the rest of the guard around and meet you at the carriage."

Galessel was ushered out the back so quickly she didn't say goodbye to the cobbler and his wife, who scurried around the shop, locking things down and grabbing bundles of supplies. She hoped the mob would leave them be.

The alley was tight—only wide enough to run through single file. Two more guards joined them, pushing them through. Clove stopped, earning her a growl from one of the guards. She huffed back, hastily pulling two pieces of black rubber from her belt pouch. She slipped them over her hooves, then nodded to the guards. They began running down the alley, Clove's hooves now silent. Galessel had to hold up her skirts to avoid tripping. The corset restricted her breathing, and she found herself becoming faint by the time they reached the dead-end.

Rosmer found the blue brick and pushed it. Nothing happened for a moment, and the guards looked around, assessing their options. Sounds of running boots near the alley nearly masked the sounds of gears clicking and a doorway opening in the wall before them. Rosmer went through first, his pistol at the ready. He signaled the all clear, and Galessel found herself pulled through the doorway by Clove, whose hand held hers in an iron grip.

The secret door opened into another alley, only this one was clean. No garbage was piled against the windowless buildings, no offal ran down the cobbles. Not even a spider web danced across the empty space. It was eerily quiet. Not even the guards' armor chimed. Galessel wasn't sure if that was because they'd silenced it or something in the alley did. She shivered. Her own breathing was loud in her ears. They ran for what seemed like several blocks, before rounding a corner into another dead-end. Another blue brick stood out in the wall, next to a small, brass-rimmed hole. Rosmer hesitantly put his eye to the hole, no doubt expecting something unpleasant to happen. Instead, he pulled his head back slowly and turned to face them, his face a portrait of surprise. "The carriage is on the other side of the door."

"Are you sure?" one of the guards behind him asked.

"You can look for yourself if you wish, but there's no mistaking the hydronium horse."

"Push the blue brick already then!" Clove's ears were flat against her head and her eyes were wide. She'd been hunted before, not long after the Great Unveiling. Running from the mob must have triggered old terrors.

Rosmer pressed the brick, waiting for the door to move, before giving a whistle that sounded just like the call of the purple night thrush. The chime of elvish armor answered. Clove pulled Galessel through the gap in the door, rushing to the carriage. Throwing open the door, Clove jumped inside, letting go of Galessel's hand at the last moment. Galessel followed her friend, but with less urgency. She found Clove huddled in the corner of the carriage, shaking. Hurrying to her, she enfolded her in a tight embrace.

"Shh. It's all right. We're safe now, Clove."

The carriage lurched forward and was soon going faster than Galessel had ever experienced in the contraption. Clove didn't stop shaking until they'd slowed to a more sedate pace. She gently pushed Galessel away.

"I'm all right now, Galey." She looked sheepish. "Thank you. I don't know what came over me."

"It is nothing to trouble yourself over, old friend. It was simply old tribulations coming back to haunt you. Your instincts merely overrode reason."

Clove huffed. "I knew things were bad in the poorer sections of Arturia, but I didn't know they'd gotten that bad. I need to expand my network."

"Is the nobility of Ashelon really behind all this?" Galessel had a difficult time comprehending how the ruling class could be so callous here. In the Hidden Lands, it was the duty of those with more privilege to aid those in need, not evict them from their homes and businesses. The only race more cruel than the humans were the Svellvega.

"It appears so, Galey. You're going to have an interesting day at court tomorrow."

Featherfoot

Chapter 4

Galessel gripped the bedpost as her maid pulled the laces of her corset tight. "Do they have to be so tight?" She gasped in between tugs. "Do the Ashelonian's require a woman to have no waist at all?"

"It would be unseemly to appear at court without an hourglass shape m'lady."

"Even an hourglass must have room to pass the grains of sand. Let me be. I can barely breathe!"

Her maid tsked, but said nothing as she tied off the corset laces and started with the petticoats.

"I much preferred the days when mortal clothing was practical and much less restrictive," Galessel grumbled, as she wormed her way into the formal gown her maids held up between them. Twice her ear charms caught on the fabric as they settled the dress over her head. *Please let this be the worst today has to offer.* Galessel knew the Goddess would not heed such pleas, but she asked anyway.

Clove arrived just as the maids were setting the last of the jeweled pins in Galessel's long braid. She may have to wear Ashelonian fashions at court, but her own traditions dictated that her ear charms be visible during any formal meeting as a sign of rank and respect for her heritage.

"Your seamstress outdid herself, Galey. That lavender silk really sets off your eyes. They look almost like amethysts."

"Good. Maybe my eyes will distract the queen from the fact that my ears are red from nearly being torn by this damnable thing." Galessel lifted the lace trimmed collar of the jacket as if it were a piece of limp lettuce and let it fall back into place. "Isn't one layer of petticoats enough? Why must another be sewn into the dress?"

Clove shrugged, laughing. Her normally flamboyant color combinations were tamed somewhat into just a pair of bright jewel tones for the visit to court. Her lemon yellow gown topped by a ruby jacket was still jarring to the eye, and yet it flattered the tawny faun. The steel of her hooves flashed beneath her skirts.

Galessel sobered. Clove's arrival meant it was nearly time to leave for her appointment with the queen. After yesterday's revealing visit, her list of topics to discuss had changed dramatically. She'd also ordered a few of her guards to take a cart full of food and other supplies down to the market before sunrise. They were to leave it in the hidden alley.

"Any news from the market?" she asked.

The smile vanished from Clove's face. "The cobbler's shop showed signs of a fire, but only on the outer wall. No one answered when Rosmer knocked on the back door. He left a note inquiring about the purchase of a pair of blue shoes in the shop. We can only hope Leatherfoot and his wife got away as easily as we did, and that they understood the message."

"Why do humans find it so hard to get along with us?"

"It's not just us, Galey. Humans can't even get along with each other. You've seen the wars they waged over nothing more than the different colors of their skin. We're different, and that's all that matters to some of them."

Galessel had seen the results of those wars. It was horrible what they did to each other over trivial differences. Truth be told, the prejudice went both ways. There were many races of fae who would have nothing to do with humans, even when their glamour had worked. She just didn't understand it. "I can only hope that Queen Victoria is sympathetic to the plight of our kin."

"You might be wishing at the wrong well, Galey. I hope you can prove me wrong."

❁　❁　❁

The carriage ride to Buckingham Palace was a quiet one. Galessel mentally rehearsed what she would say to the queen; all thoughts of trade agreements and coffee shipments were long since forgotten. Clove sat quietly, letting her brood, knowing the importance of this meeting. Galessel was grateful to her friend for that.

The rank air from the city seeped in past the carriage

door, and Galessel was thankful for once that her corset wouldn't let her take a deep breath, as they bounced over the uneven cobbles. She couldn't shake the feeling that this wasn't going to go well. Miniel had warned her that Victoria had become increasingly intolerant of any criticism of her or her policies. Her sister speculated, as did many others, that Victoria's sudden conversion to the worship of Asher, the god of chaos and strife, was to blame. Many human rulers had converted to his worship over the last fifty years, most hoping their obeisance would spare their countries from any future comet strikes. The continent of Zorrovia still hadn't recovered.

The bouncing stopped as the carriage swayed to a stop. The door opened, and a surprisingly fresh breeze threatened to steal her hat. Galessel stepped out onto the artfully manicured white gravel path before the palace. Secure behind a wrought iron fence and yards of emerald green grass, her guards stood ready but relaxed at her side. Sounds of a protest reached her ears and she turned toward the street. Humans marched before the palace gates with signs. Some read, "Monsters go home!" while others bore pictures of fae burning in effigy. Her stomach knotted a little tighter.

"Are protests like these common, Clove?"

"They've been growing in number recently, yes."

A rotten apple bounced across the grass, rolling to a stop at the edge of the gravel. Galessel's guards closed in around her.

"We should go inside, Your Highness, let the palace guards deal with these ruffians," Daylor said, as he looked pointedly at a red-coated, Ashelonian guard. The guard looked straight ahead, clearly ignoring what he deemed a non-threat.

She nodded, exchanging concerned looks with Clove. Several more projectiles landed on the gravel, but Galessel refused to look behind her. She strode into the palace as if nothing were amiss.

CHAPTER 5

As Galessel and her companions made their way through the huge, carved double doors leading into the marble covered antechamber of Buckingham Palace, the human need for opulence affronted her senses. Heavy velvet tapestries hung all along the walls of the rectangular room depicting scenes of glorious battles and fantastical creatures. Spaced between the tapestries were several marble statues of long-dead Ashelonian monarchs, each standing ten feet tall. Milling about at various small tables or seated in wonderfully carved wooden chairs were nobles from all over the world. They looked like fragile, brightly colored birds the way they fluttered about the hall, and the mix of perfumes and nosegays were enough to drive a bloodhound mad.

In all of the splendor and opulence, not a single other fae was present. With all that she'd seen the past few days, she wasn't surprised.

Determined not to show any weakness, she held her head high, setting her face in a visage of confidence and royal bearing. Heads turned as she entered, and she could feel the courtiers' eyes on her. She wished Clove were at her side, but the faun had taken her leave soon after entering the palace, claiming a need to meet with persons unknown. While she did not doubt her friend's word, she also knew how much Clove disliked dealing with royalty, herself excluded, of course.

Galessel took a deep breath, settling into her role. She was an ambassador. She'd negotiated with trolls and traded ritual insults with dwarves. Walking through a room full of humans should be easy. So why was she so nervous?

Her butterflies were temporarily quelled by the approach of a kindly dowager in a black dress. She used a cane, but a young dandy in a bright blue suit stood close by her elbow, his body tense and ready to aid her at the slightest stumble.

"Good day!" The dowager's voice was stronger than her frail body inferred. "You must be Princess Galessel."

Galessel nodded, thinking quickly through her sister's list of notable nobles. "I am. Do I have the honor of greeting Dame Blankenship?"

The old woman beamed and held out her hand. "You do, child. Tell me how is your sister? Has she had her child?"

She took the offered hand, holding it lightly, afraid the poor woman might crumble at the barest jostle. "She is well. When last I saw her, she was pacing along the garden paths, imploring the Goddess to deliver her child sooner rather than later."

The Dame laughed. "Children will come when they want, gods be damned." Her companion gasped at the blasphemy. She gave him a withering look. "I should know. I have nine of mine own."

"You have been truly blessed, Dame Blankenship. Please forgive me, but I must make my way to the chamberlain. If it would please you, I'd be honored to have you to tea later this week. My sister speaks very highly of you."

"Oh, that would be delightful! Have one of your servants come by the manor with the date." Dame Blankenship gave her a nod and made to depart. "Don't worry about meeting the queen, dear. She can be a bit of a prude, but you'll do just fine."

The old woman toddled off, her companion lecturing her on propriety. Galessel thought she heard the elderly dame tell him where he could put his advice. She smiled. That woman had spirit.

Greeting the other nobles came easier after her conversation with Lady Blankenship. She wasn't sure if it was her confidence returning or the apparent approval of the dame, but other nobles sought her out as she made her way toward the chamberlain stationed near the entrance to the queen's receiving room. She made a mental note to thank her sister for the exhaustive list of nobles she'd made her memorize for just this purpose.

Nearing the chamberlain, a glint of gold caught her eye. Her sister had told her that ear adornments were becoming more popular here, but humans preferred to wear jewelry on their lobes, not at the top of their ears.

She looked through the crowd, and her heart skipped a beat. Talking to a noble from Hellas was a Svellvega elf, his gold earring shining in the top of his ear. Her guards followed her gaze and began to draw their swords. Before they could attract attention to themselves, she held out a shaking hand, whispering, "Stay your hands."

Daylor growled, but slid his sword back into its scabbard, his hand staying on the hilt. "The Svellvega should not be here, Your Highness. We should leave. Something is amiss."

"I agree that something is amiss, but if we leave, we will not discover what it is. I will meet with the queen as planned."

The slowness with which her guards pulled their hands from their swords spoke volumes about their displeasure, but they nodded and stepped closer to her. She looked for the enemy elf, but he'd melted back into the crowd. Her heart raced at the thought of her land's enemies openly present in Ashelon. Were they here scouting for an invasion, as they'd lobbied to do centuries ago before they moved north, or were they seeking to ally themselves with Ashelon? The possibilities and ramifications of each scenario tumbled in her head as she neared the throne room, barely registering the continued greetings from the nobles she passed.

The chamberlain spied her, motioning Galessel to approach, concluding his conversation with a pompous dandy in an oversized top hat and emerald green coat as she did so. His face was a mask, but his eyes betrayed a hint of disdain as he silently appraised her. His glance lasted only a moment before he bowed over her hand.

"Princess Galessel, is it a pleasure to have you at court."

"Thank you, my Lord Chamberlain. I am honored to be here to represent my people."

The chamberlain looked pointedly at Galessel's guards. "Forgive me, Your Highness, but your sister must have failed to mention that your guards are not allowed in the queen's audience chamber. I'm afraid they'll have to wait outside."

She could sense her guards' hands hovering near their sword hilts. She wanted desperately to use her gift to convince the man to let them go with her, especially after spying the Svellvega, but she dare not.

"Forgive my guards, my lord. They are overprotective of me—used to guarding me from fearsome beings in the Hidden Lands." She paused for a moment, willfully holding back her gift. "If they left their weapons out here, would you permit them to remain at my side?"

The chamberlain eyed her guards, gauging whether they would be a threat. He motioned for two nearby palace guards to approach. They were heavily armed, not only with swords, but also with the latest hand-held, hydronium-powered firearms.

"That would be an acceptable compromise. James, collect their weapons." As the guard moved forward to disarm the elven guards, the chamberlain returned his attention to Galessel. "Two of the palace guard will escort you as well. To assure your safety."

It was a barely concealed threat, but without using her gift, it was an acceptable compromise. "Thank you, my lord. You are most generous."

The chamberlain gave her a slight bow. As he rose, the doors to the queen's receiving room opened and a most curious creature, followed by an elegantly attired gentleman, exited the room. Lion-like in shape and form, it was an entirely mechanical construct made of highly polished brass. Steam-powered pistons hissed as the creature's legs moved, and the ticking of internal clockwork could be clearly heard in the now silent antechamber. Deliberate movement of its head, as if it were evaluating which noble to have for lunch, made it seem alive. Only the small metal rod protruding from its head, coupled with the small box in the gentleman's hand with a similar rod, betrayed that it was not in actuality moving of its own free will.

Galessel whispered to the chamberlain as the pair passed them by, "Is he controlling that creature without wires?"

The chamberlain merely nodded, too fascinated with the construct to say anything else.

Whispers expanded into more animated talk, as the gentleman with the mechanical lion exited the anteroom. The construct was impressive, to be sure, but Galessel knew of several tinkers who had built much more awe-inspiring constructs.

The chamberlain startled her from her thoughts, as he resumed his duties, motioning to the still open doors. "Her Majesty will see you now, Princess."

Taking a deep breath, she squared her shoulders and walked into destiny.

Victoria

Chapter 6

Galessel stepped through the doors into the Wessex Room, the queen's grand office where she most often met with foreign dignitaries. A lush Persian rug in desert hues covered most of the white marble floor. Gold silk curtains spun by centaurs from the finest silk of the Hidden Lands framed two large windows, which let in the weak Arturian sun, providing light should the queen wish to sit at the large roll-top desk set between them.

Bits and bobbles from around the world decorated small tables scattered around the room. A small fire burned in the office's fireplace, and small paintings of the royal family graced the mantle, in full view of the golden couch placed in front of it. Two flags flanked the fireplace: the Union Jack on a brass pole on the left, and a red flag with Asher's symbol in black—a circle with eight arrows pointing out around a single teardrop— hung from a black pole on the right. Though not as opulent as the antechamber, it was obvious the room, and everything in it, was designed to impress visitors. Galessel could almost feel the weight of the words and decisions that had been made in this room over the years.

Galessel's guards followed her into the room, taking up positions on either side of the door where they were flanked by the queen's own guards. In this smaller space, the tension between the opposing men was palpable. She prayed her own would keep their cool. They would be no match against the firearms the Ashelonian guards carried.

"Your Majesty, Princess Galessel Avandi, Ambass- ador of the Hidden Lands," the chamberlain announced, before bowing and returning to the anteroom, closing the doors quietly as he did so.

Queen Victoria sat in a high-backed chair near the fire, drumming her fingers on its thick wooden arm. Her makeup could not hide the signs of stress from ruling half the known world, even though she was barely thirty years of age. Galessel tried not to wrinkle her nose at the noxious mix of too much perfume and body odor that wafted not only from the queen, but also from the two retainers standing quietly near the back of the room. She never understood the human's lack of desire for basic hygiene. Curtseying, Galessel waited to be acknowledged by Ashelon's ruler.

A bare nod of the head was the only acknowledgement given by the human queen for several minutes. Obviously sizing her up, Victoria tapped a finger on the arm of her throne, the ring upon it flashing with a blue fire found only in ice diamonds. Exceptionally rare, they were known to possess the ability to protect the wearer from magical influence. Galessel was not surprised to see something of its like upon Victoria's hand, but the fact that the Svellvega's lands were the only source of those diamonds made her breath catch in her throat. What exactly was going on in Ashelon?

Victoria noticed the direction of Galessel's stare and

broke her silence. "Your sister speaks highly of you and says you are a capable diplomat. How find you our fair city?"

It was curious that Victoria said nothing about the ring, given her pointed glance, but Galessel decided instead to pursue the opening to talk about the conditions in the city.

"As you know, it has been several decades since I've visited the mortal realms. Your city has grown much in that time and is very impressive." The queen nodded, smiling slightly. "However, the condition of your people, and those from the Hidden Lands, leaves much to be desired, if I may be so bold, Your Highness."

"Treating with trolls has dulled your sense of propriety, it seems. One does not often hear insults to one's city on an introductory visit."

"Forgive me, Your Majesty, but I can be nothing but honest. I have encountered humans and fae alike, living in abhorrent conditions, many of whom claimed to have been removed from their homes and businesses for no reason other than being fae or associating with us. I thought the animosity of the Faerie Riots was long behind us."

"Though I was a child when the treaties were signed, I remember well that one condition your mother agreed to was that the Hidden Lands would not interfere in the governance of Ashelon. Are you questioning how I govern my empire?" Victoria leaned forward in her chair, her face reddening.

Galessel, well schooled on the various treaties the Hidden Lands held with the mortal realms, fired back, "The treaty also states that all peoples, whether mortal or fae, would be treated equally."

"And they have. I presume you were referring to evictions in a section of the West End?" Galessel nodded. "Everyone, fae or otherwise, was relocated for a new transportation project." Victoria sat back in her throne. A smile like a cat with a mouse firmly under its paw spread across her face. "You see, if you'd bothered to do even a little bit of reading in the papers, you would have known that a team of scientists has developed a new tunneling engine, and that neighborhood in the West End will be the site of a new underground railway station. The Underground will revolutionize travel within the city."

Clove never mentioned a new transportation system, and neither did anyone she'd talked to near the market.

It wasn't adding up. "Be that as it may, evicting those people without recompense is unjust."

One of the queen's retainers gasped, and a deeper voice chuckled, while the queen's visage grew visibly darker. "Without recompense? They were relocated to perfectly good homes nearer the market and given a hundred pounds sterling. I would consider that generous recompense."

Was that what her underlings had told her, or was she lying? Galessel didn't know enough about Victoria to know for sure, so she pressed on.

"Forgive me, Your Majesty, but either you are ignorant of what 'perfectly good' means to a common soul, or you have been deceived as to the actual disposition of those people. Their homes are barely more than hovels, their businesses are in ruins, and none mentioned anything of a stipend."

Queen Victoria sat up straight, then leaned forward slightly. Galessel heard the clank of Ashelonian armor as the queen's guards stepped forward, followed swiftly by the chime of her own guards' steps.

"Again you insult me? And so blatantly! What do you hope to gain by such insolence?"

Miniel had counseled her to choose her words carefully with Victoria. Apparently even a slight implication of naïveté was too much. She might regret it later, but honesty wasn't something she was used to holding back.

"I seek to protect and aid those less fortunate than I. The Hidden Lands exports food, building materials, and goods to aid your people and the fae who live here, and have since before the Great Unveiling. In my realm it is the duty of all to aid those with less privilege so that we all may grow as a people. But what I have witnessed in my few days here tells me that your realm does not uphold the same ideals."

The queen sputtered, her face nearly turning purple. Galessel knew she'd overstepped her bounds and would soon be thrown out, but before she could try to calm the indignant monarch, a pastel-skinned elf materialized from the shadows near the fireplace. Like many of his race, his skin was of the palest blue, and he wore his black hair long and tied back at the nape of his neck. A black velvet top hat adorned his head, and a golden earring caught the light in the tip of his ear. A jeweled eye patch over his right eye, coupled with a broad smile, set Galessel in mind of an ice wolf who had just spotted its prey. Her heart skipped a beat and her hand flew to her chest. She knew her guards reached for swords they no longer had. Finding herself taking a step backward, she stopped, fighting the instinct to run.

"I told you, Your Majesty, that the Anisbarii have no stomach for progress," the Svellvega said with a sneer. He stepped farther into the light, nearly even with the queen's chair, and flipped back the long edge of his black coat, revealing a small hydronium cannon in a holster strapped to his thigh.

Victoria said nothing, smiling at Galessel's discomfiture.

Galessel didn't know what to say. A thousand things skittered through her brain, but only a small percentage of them was anything other than to run or fight.

In an odd turn, the Svellvega bowed with a deep flourish. As he straightened, he said, "As I do not wish to be rude, please allow me to introduce myself, Princess. I am Lord Davorin, envoy of the grand republic of the Svellvega."

Refusing to give the lord even the barest of nods, she returned her gaze to Victoria, who sat comfortably reclined in her chair once again. "Your Majesty, the

Anisbarii and the Svellvega have been enemies for hundreds of years. They are ruthless mercenaries and pirates. I would entreat you to reconsider whatever dealings you have with them, if you value the safety of your realm."

Victoria laughed. It was not a pretty sound. "And what would you say if I told you that Lord Davorin has said the same thing about you? That you have been deceiving us, and using mind control to maintain an upper hand in negotiations?"

Gentle Goddess. Clove must have been right about that spy. Is that why the Svellvega gifted her an ice diamond? Her family had never used the silver tongue gifts to gain the advantage against Ashelon, but there would be no way to convince Victoria of that. She had to try though. "Your Majesty, I assure you, no mind control magic has ever been used by our ambassadors. It would be dishonorable, and is against our laws."

"And yet why do I only now wear proof against such magic? As allies, I would have thought you would wish to protect us against such things. Why not give us a gift such as this yourself?" She held up the hand with the ice diamond ring again for emphasis.

Victoria had a point. Though incredibly rare, the royal family did possess a few of the gems. She would have to stretch the truth just a little to counter it. "Why would one need protection against something that is so rare among my people that those with the ability are only born every few hundred years? You would never need such a gift in your lifetime."

"She lies, Your Majesty," Lord Davorin said without a hint of emotion. "Not two days ago, a compatriot of mine witnessed the princess using magic to coerce a group of people to leave the market. It has long been rumored that she inherited the silver tongue from her grandmother, and now we know it to be truth."

The barest flick of Victoria's fingers, and a pair of Ashelonian guards were by her side. Galessel glanced over her shoulder to find her own guards flanked, as well. She could use her gift to get past the guards, but she'd only prove Davorin's point for him. Maybe it was time to go on the offensive.

"Lord Davorin speaks nothing but hearsay." She glared at the Svellvega a moment before looking pointedly at Victoria's ice diamond. "And while the ice diamond may protect you from magical influence by myself or others, it may not protect you from the Svellvega. I'm sure the esteemed lord failed to mention they can be attuned to allow specific magics to pass unhindered."

Victoria looked to Davorin who gave the barest shake of his head. "You counter an accusation of lying with more lies? We regret the loss of your sister to us due to her condition, and we regret your mother's choice to send you in her stead even more. We will stomach your presence here no longer. When you return home, inform your mother that your replacement must not be from the royal family. We will no longer be unduly influenced by elven magic."

As Galessel's arms were enclosed in paired iron grips, she held her ground, refusing to be ushered to the door. "Your Majesty, you're making a dire mistake! The Svellvega cannot be trusted. You would throw away decades of goodwill between our peoples for the honeyed lies of that pirate?"

"Given the choice between imports of second-rate textiles and foods and an ally with a full standing army willing to aid us in defense of our empire, I will choose the security of my realm every time, Princess. You are dismissed."

Galessel was pulled forcefully toward the door. She attempted to shake off the queen's guards, saying, "I am perfectly capable of walking out of here on my own, thank you." The guards looked to the queen before letting her go. Her guards, however, were forcefully hauled out of the room.

As the door slammed behind them, the chamberlain approached, his hand held up. The Ashelonian guards stopped, still holding Galessel's struggling guards. "The princess's carriage is at the west entrance. Her guards are not to be released until you are outside the palace."

She would not be escorted through the palace like a common criminal. She'd done nothing wrong. The chamberlain wasn't wearing any ice diamonds. She lowered her eyes so no one would see them flash, and let her anger fuel her will. "This is an outrage, Lord Smythe. We are not a threat. Release my guards and allow us to leave peacefully."

The chamberlain's eyes turned silver for just a moment. He bowed in apology and motioned for the queen's guards to release hers. They did so very reluctantly, never moving from their positions.

"Forgive me, Your Highness. The safety of the palace is my men's utmost concern. They will escort you and your men to your carriage, and their weapons will be sent via courier to your townhouse."

She turned on her heels and walked from the room flanked by the queen's guards. Whispers and the chime of her guards' armor followed in her wake.

davbrin

Chapter 7

Clove was already in the carriage when Galessel returned, and she noticed her friend's distress immediately. "Galey, what happened?" she asked.

Galessel shook her head. Where to start? With the Svellvega? Being dismissed? Or the fact that in a single day she'd managed to nearly destroy fifty years of open relations with Ashelon? Tears started to fall, and she was powerless to stop them. "I don't know where to start," she told her friend between sobs.

Clove moved to sit next to Galessel, putting her arm around her shoulders. "Start at the beginning?"

Galessel laughed weakly, and dabbed at her eyes with a handkerchief before beginning her tale. She condensed it as much as she could, but Clove kept interrupting her for details about what the Svellvega elves looked like and how the queen reacted when Davorin spoke.

"Why does it matter?" she asked Clove, annoyed with the latest interrogation about Davorin. "He's Svellvega and apparently a lord, though they don't use ear rings like we do. I don't understand why you care what kind of jewelry he was wearing."

"Because if he gave the queen an ice diamond, he probably had a twin, cut from the same crystal on him somewhere. If he had similar abilities to yours, he'd have one. In close proximity, the twin diamonds would cancel each other out, and he could use magic to influence Victoria."

That gave Galessel pause. She closed her eyes, searching her memories for any sign of an ice diamond on the Svellvega lord. He'd kept to the shadows mostly, his hands in his pockets. "I don't know. If he had one, he kept it hidden." Galessel gave her friend a sideways glance. "How did you know about the twin diamond effect? I'd never heard of it."

Clove gave her a guilty look, her ears falling. "It's only something that's recently come to light. A, uh, friend of mine heard rumors. Said a Skanish mage had obtained a pair and was doing some research."

Sighing, Galessel sat back on her bench and looked up at the roof of the carriage. "I find it hard to believe that Victoria would willingly treat with the Svellvega, and while I also can't put too much stock in rumors, too much is coming together. The presence of the Svellvega at court, the rumors in the paper this morning. I have to assume that the queen does, in fact, have her heart set on conquering the Hidden Lands, among other places, and most likely with the Svellvega's help." Galessel thought for a moment. "I need to get back to the Hidden Lands as soon as possible."

Clove snorted, her version of spitting in revulsion. "Treating with the Svellvega will be a double-edged sword for Victoria, whether it's by magical influence or not. You can't trust elves who live on a Goddess-forsaken ice-locked isle, filled with the most dangerous beasts in either realm. They'll help her all right, and then they'll turn around and kill her once she's served her purpose, just like they do with everyone else."

"We can only hope they turn on her before she attempts to conquer the Hidden Lands, Goddess forgive me for saying so," Galessel replied, surprised at her own spite.

Clove nodded her agreement and bowed her head in a quick prayer to Donnan, the Goddess of Fate. Raising her head, she brushed her hands over opposite shoulders in a sign meant to clear away unwanted webs of destiny.

Galessel did the same, praying she was wrong about Victoria and her motives.

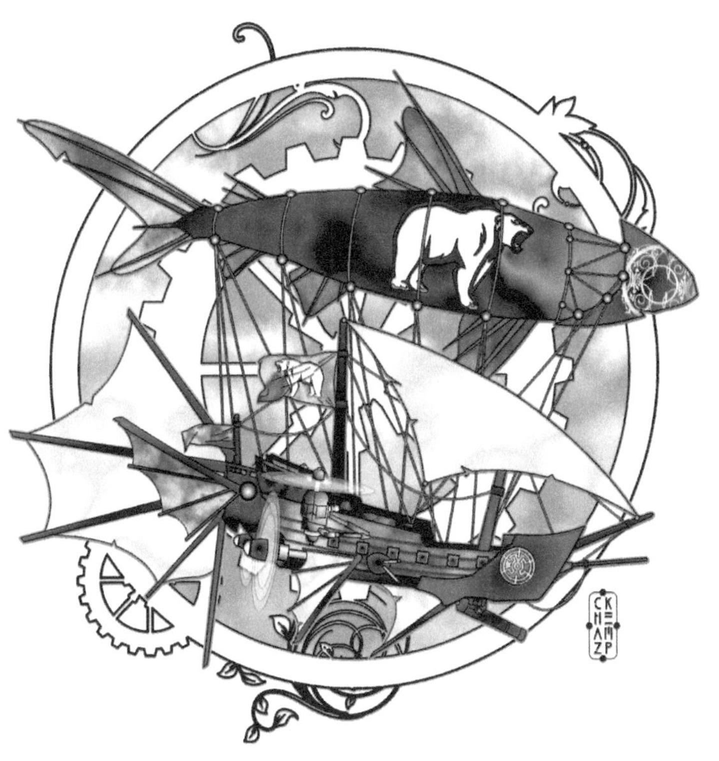

Chapter 8

A warning bell sounded, its harsh jangle startling Galessel from her thoughts. They'd only been in the air for a few hours. Was there something wrong with the ship? She'd gone straight to the airfield after her meeting with Victoria, leaving Clove behind to gather more information. And though their departure had been hasty, N'hena had been prepared. Setting her book down, she stood to look out the porthole. Her cabin was positioned nearest the bow with a view out the port side. Members of N'hena's crew ran past, some with guns in their hands. Crossing the short distance to the cabin door, she opened it to find Garrik and Daylor standing with their swords drawn on either side of the door, alert and ready for trouble.

Garrick, looking over his shoulder at her, said grimly, "Well, Your Highness, it looks like our trip has just become interesting."

Before Galessel could reply, Daylor quipped back, "Leave it to you, brother, to make the word 'interesting' sound like a curse."

Galessel smiled at her guards' banter. The twins were easygoing under normal circumstances, but they were more than willing to sacrifice their lives for the safety of their princess; they would not have passed the trials to become royal bodyguards otherwise.

N'hena could be heard over the ship's voice amplifier barking orders. "Kirkly, keep an eye on those hydronium levels! Winston, prepare for a rapid ascent on my mark! Sally, it's time to test out your new steam-powered propellers. Looks like we're going to need them. All hands! Prepare to repel boarders."

As the *Intrepid's* crew rushed to obey their captain's orders, Galessel stepped from her cabin to the rail to see what was causing the alarm. An airship was approaching from behind. Even at this distance it was visibly larger than the *Intrepid*. The ship's imposing all-black exterior made it appear as if the whole thing were made of hard, northern wynterwood. A shiver ran down her spine, and she tightened her grip on the polished teak of the rail. The black airship was gaining quickly, the image on its balloon becoming clearer: a roaring snow bear with bloody claws—the symbol of her race's long-time enemy. A longer study of the approaching ship confirmed her fears. The crew had spiked black hair and gold rings puncturing the tips of their pointed ears. They were Svellvega.

She jumped at Daylor's gentle touch on her shoulder. "Your Highness, you should return to your cabin. It's not safe for you out here."

Galessel followed Daylor into her cabin and took a step toward the small window to continue watching. She immediately felt a strong grip upon her arm.

"That would not be wise, Your Highness," Garrik said from behind her.

Positioning themselves to block all possible entry to her cabin, her two guards filled the small but well-appointed room, making Galessel feel slightly claustrophobic. Knowing they would brook no protest from her, she resigned herself to finding a comfortable seated position on her bed. The human corset and bustle, however, made that endeavor near to impossible. She silently cursed herself for not changing into more comfortable clothes when she first got on board, but she'd been too preoccupied, playing her meeting with Victoria over and over in her mind.

The shouting outside increased, and Galessel could hear the amplified voices of the Svellvega elves demanding the *Intrepid* surrender and prepare for boarding. N'hena refused, yelling curses through her own voice amplifier at the raiders in a variety of languages. After a brief pause in her tirade, N'hena yelled, "Sally, now!"

Galessel and her guards heard a loud hiss, and then the ship jerked. They rose quickly and her stomach dropped. Those new steam-powered propellers N'hena was so proud of seemed to be working perfectly.

As the din outside quieted down, Galessel wondered if they'd managed to outrun the black ship. Garrick glared at her, as she pushed herself off the bed to get a better view out the window. The next moment, with the terrifying scream of an elven-wrought cannonball, he was simply gone. The smell of sulfur from spent gunpowder permeated the air, and the sun blazed through a gaping hole in the outer wall of her cabin. Bits of wood and what felt like rain peppered her skin. She pushed herself off the bed where she'd fallen, and turned toward her door to discover Daylor was gone as well, along with the door and a large chunk of the wall of the cabin across the hall. Galessel turned around in shock, wondering where her guards had gone, then realized the whole cabin was bathed in red. She looked down at her hands. She screamed and tried in vain to wipe the blood from her hands.

Two large, fur-clad Svellvega elves rushed through the hole in her cabin wall. The fall of their boots on the wooden deck sounded like muffled thumps. They grinned at each other and charged toward her. Galessel looked around the room for anything she could use as a weapon.

"Well, look what we have here, an Anisbarii whore," the Svellvega with a particularly large gold ring through his left ear tip whispered.

"And all dressed up like her human whore-masters, too," the other replied just as quietly.

Galessel couldn't understand why they were whispering. Wasn't there a battle going on? Maybe this was a dream. It had to be. She'd fallen asleep while reading and her mind was telling a horrific story. This would be a good time to wake up.

But the dream didn't end. Galessel's heart faltered at the look of pure hatred when she met their eyes. As the two elves rushed her, she reached for the lamp on the bedside table—an ornate affair with a solid brass stand and a stained glass shade. It wouldn't budge. Like most things on a ship, it was bolted down. Frantic, she spotted her copy of *Gulliver's Travels* on the chair. She reached for it, flinging it at the nearest Svellvega. It bounced off his chest. He glanced down as the book hit the floor, but kept coming. He grabbed her wrists, slamming her body against the wall of her cabin, pinning her arms above her head. His breath smelled of rotten fish.

"Hold her down on the bed, Skathis, while I dock the *gorsekanna's* ears," the Svellvega with the thick gold hoop through his ear tip said to his underling, whose earring was much thinner, indicating a lesser rank. Leering at Galessel, he said, "Since you're obviously so in love with your human masters, why don't we make you look like one?"

Galessel struggled as Skathis, the underling, pulled her from the wall. Her kicks landed on legs padded with thick fur. Her captor grinned, showing sharpened teeth. He picked her up by her wrists and threw her on the bed. She tried to get up and run, but the damned corset restricted her movement. Skathis laughed, pouncing on her like some great bear. His meaty hands took her arms in a bruising grip, and he planted his knee in the middle of her chest. She struggled to breathe.

She'd heard stories all of her life of how savage the Svellvega were. She'd never quite believed any elf could be that uncivilized. Her ears began to ring, but she pushed the sound to the back of her mind, determined to put an end to this foul treatment.

"Do this thing and there will be war between our peoples!" she said, indignant. She thrashed, trying to pull her arms from Skathis' grip. Her wrists were damp with blood and slipped just a little. Skathis tightened his grip. She felt something in her wrists pop with a burst of pain. She couldn't help the yelp that escaped her throat. Skathis leered at her, his joy in her pain sparking a flame of anger. "I am Galessel, Thrice Daughter of Queen Thessalia. I demand that you unhand me!" Using her innate talent, she willed her words to have an effect.

The elf with the large earring spat on the floor, as he drew a wicked-looking knife from his belt. "Will be war? Have you been living under a barrow your entire life, Princess?"

His laugh made her skin crawl. Galessel's heart sank. Using her silver tongue to sway people with her words rarely worked on elves, but it had been worth trying. She tried to buck Skathis off of her, but the effort only earned her a cuff to the side of her head and a knee deeper in her ribs. The room wobbled and the ringing in her ears increased to the point where she could barely hear what the other elf was saying.

"We've been at war ever since your grandparents forced us to move north." He turned to the opening in the wall and called out, "Korris! Get in here. We've found us quite the prize."

Leaning over Galessel, the elf leader fingered the edge on his blade, as another black-haired Svellvega entered the room. "Korris, search the room. I'll bet she has a stash of those sun crystals hidden around here somewhere. These *madlas* never go anywhere without those. While you do that, I'm gonna fix this *bidjwa's* ears."

Korris eyed her with lust in his ice blue eyes before doing as he was told. Sun crystals were worth a fortune on the black market, but he wouldn't find any. Only mystics used them anymore.

Bent backward over the bed, Galessel shuddered as the one with the large earring shoved her head to the side and grabbed the tip of her ear hard enough to bend the wires of her charms.

"Can I have her after you're done, captain?" Korris asked, as he tossed the contents of Galessel's steamer trunk on the floor.

"I don't know why you'd want to sully yourself with an Anisbarii, but go ahead. They won't claim her after I'm done with her," the captain laughed, the sound turning Galessel's insides to water.

Cold steel against her ear turned quickly to fire, as the captain sliced into the top of her ear. The mark of her rank as princess would be the first to go. How could this be happening? Where were her guards? Galessel closed her eyes against the pain and screamed. Her guards were gone. She was alone. Her heart felt like it was trying to beat its way out of her throat. She tried to move her head, to move away from the fire slicing into her ear, but she couldn't. The Svellvega pushed her head further into the mattress and cut deeper. The sound of the knife cutting cartilage made her retch. The captain laughed and continued with his work, cutting slowly, savoring the pain he caused. Every ragged slice of the knife sent jolts of lightning through her whole body.

"You Anisbarii and your ear charms." The Svellvega laughed, as he dangled the scholar's ring, still encased in bloody flesh, in front of her face. "I'm gonna cut each one out, and by the time I'm done, you'll look just like one of your pretty little humans."

The captain, done with her left ear, grabbed her face with a meaty hand, his thick nails digging into her cheeks, and turned her head to the other side. Blood pooled beneath her cheek, and a new form of agony erupted, as he pushed her head back into the bed.

Each new cut of the knife stripped a piece of her identity away; all signs of her accomplishments, skills, and lineage dropped to the floor with every ring torn from her ears. She screamed until her throat was so raw it felt like the Svellvega had taken his knife to her throat.

Tears streamed down her cheeks, mixing with the blood from her ears. She'd failed on so many levels on this trip, and now, now she was as good as faceless. How would she ever be able to face her family, much less the beings of the Hidden Lands, whom she was supposed to serve? They'd never trust her now.

Casually tossing a piece of her ear out of the hole in the ruined cabin wall, he straightened, saying, "Now, that's better, isn't it?" His smile never reached his ice blue eyes.

Exhausted and defeated, Galessel could do nothing more than whimper. Her entire head throbbed and her ears were engulfed in dragon fire.

"Boys, finish up here, but be quick about it. We're leaving just as soon as I find that sylph and rip her wings off."

As the captain left, he held one gold ring with an amethyst dangling from it up to the light—the ring marking her as the ambassador to the humans. "I think I might keep this one."

Everything she was, everything she worked for, was now gone. Tossed over the rail, or in the stinking, meaty palm of her enemy. A wracking sob earned her a rough shake that jostled her head and inflamed her ears even more.

Skathis continued to hold her down, giving Korris an annoyed look when he finally took their captain's place.

"You're mine now Anisbarii wh—"

The tip of a cutlass ripped through Korris' chest before he could finish. From behind them, twin gunshots rang out, as Korris grabbed at the cutlass blade protruding through him. He fell to his knees, and the weight lifted from Galessel's limbs as her captor crumpled to the floor.

N'hena wiped the blood from her sword and sheathed it, kicked the body of the elven pirate aside, and reached out to help Galessel sit up. She gasped at the sight before her, her wings flashing from an angry red to a sick-looking green.

"Call the medic, Clive, and be quick about it!" N'hena yelled at her first mate, who was holstering his smoking pistols.

He took in the scene before him, his face turning white, then green, before running from the room to fetch the ship's doctor.

"By the Old Ones, Princess, what have they done to

you?" N'hena gently turned Galessel's head from one side to the other, her face blanching to match her wings. "Your beautiful ears. Dear Goddess. I—" N'hena looked away for a moment, taking a shaking breath before turning to face Galessel once more. "I don't know how we'll fix this, Princess, but I swear I won't rest 'til we catch that Svellvega scum and feed him to an agar roch."

Shaking with shock and pain that throbbed in time with her racing heart, Galessel bowed her head in shame. How could she ever return home after this?

"There is no fixing this, N'hena," she sobbed, her voice hoarse. "They have inflicted on me the *Dien-Vek*: a punishment so severe, none in generations of my people have endured it." Memories of her grandmother's stories whispered in her mind, telling her of the horrors that would face her if she disobeyed her elders—the horrors of no longer being an elf. It was several long moments before she could continue. "I am nothing now. My identity is gone. Everything I have worked for lies in bloody pieces on the floor. They have removed my ear tips and branded me *sikevra*. An outcast."

CHAPTER 9

Princess Galessel looked in the mirror, her hands reaching tentatively toward the bandages on her ears but stopping short. Curiosity warred with revulsion. What would her ears look like now? She knew they wouldn't be softly rounded like a human's— she forbade the doctors from doing that when they ministered to her after the attack. She would rather have horribly disfigured ears than ones that made her look like a human, but the mere thought of no longer having graceful points at the tops of her ears brought tears to her eyes. She'd always loved the look of her ears, the soft inside arc, and way the points parted her raven hair when she wore it down. Her ears had been her only vanity.

Though two weeks has passed since the attack, it felt like only yesterday. Every time she looked in the mirror, she felt violated, less of an elf. Docking of the ears was a punishment her people reserved for only the most heinous of crimes. But she hadn't done anything wrong, and that made the violation even worse.

The royal doctor ordered her to leave the bandages on for at least another week. Her mother admonished her daily to leave them be and let them heal as best they could. Galessel was unsure if she could leave the bandages on for much longer. Her ears itched with healing, and her hands longed to rip the bandages from her ears to see their destruction for herself.

Galessel clutched her hands around her middle as she paced in front of the mirror. She feared the worst: that she'd be shunned within the Hidden Lands for the rest of her life.

Unfortunately, magic couldn't heal her ears. The pieces carved from them were lost in the chaotic aftermath of the attack on the *Intrepid*. Galessel didn't blame N'hena or her crew for the loss. If it weren't for them, the pirates would have done much worse. No, she put all of the blame on the Svellvega.

In the days of Galessel's great-great-grandparents, the Svellvega were a small tribe of elves who held to a fierce belief in survival of the fittest. For reasons unknown, they moved north to an island completely covered in ice, and the harsh weather cut them off from the rest of the Hidden Lands for eleven months of the year. There they stayed, isolated, for nearly five hundred years.

Then the raids started. Small ones at first on the more remote reaches of the Hidden Lands, but the Svellvega grew bolder, and the raids increased in frequency and ferocity. After the massacre of an entire village of gnomes, the Anisbarii sent an envoy of twenty skilled diplomats to the Svellvega stronghold. Only one returned, months later.

His tale was one of initial acceptance followed by betrayal. The Svellvega treated the envoys as honored guests for many days before all pretense was dropped and they were thrown into an icy pit and forced to battle an ice bear for their lives with nothing but their bare hands. The surviving diplomat had been kept in chains and forced to watch the entire ordeal, then sent back to deliver the Svellvega's ultimatum. Kill, or be killed. The Svellvega vowed to continue their raids and would give no quarter.

In the years that followed, the Anisbarii fought the Svellvega, delivering several deciding defeats to the survivalist elves. The Svellvega attacks ceased after a failed raid, in which all of the Svellvega attackers were killed. Many thought that was the last of the Svellvega, while others surmised they'd simply gone back home to regroup and rebuild their numbers. Now they knew the latter was true.

As Galessel gazed in the mirror, she whispered, "Someday, you filthy pirates, I will pay you back." But how? How could she gain her revenge when she had no skills in the fighting arts? She was a princess and an ambassador trained in negotiation and court intrigue, not a warrior skilled with the blade or gun.

"Come away from the mirror, my daughter," Galessel's mother, Queen Thessalia, said as she entered the bedchamber.

Galessel saw her own eyes in her mother's, but she

got her dark locks from her father. Even in the privacy of their own rooms, her mother's bearing was regal, though her dappled blue eyes shone with unshed tears.

Galessel looked away from their reflections, unable to bear the look of pity in her mother's eyes. "Have you and Father discussed who will replace me in Victoria's court?" she asked, hoping to forestall any talk of her ears.

Her mother took a loosely woven silk shawl from the back of Galessel's reading chair and held it out to her. "Come, it's a beautiful day. If you insist on discussing politics, let's at least do it while we walk in the gardens."

Galessel took the shawl, dyed the royal blue of her House's colors, and smiled at her mother in thanks. It was time to face not only what had happened at court, but also what had befallen her afterward. Galessel pulled the shawl around her shoulders and followed her mother out of the room.

Galessel admired the colorful blossoms that draped from overhanging branches and sprung out of the ground in plush carpets that lined the stone pathway. Birds sang and played in carved fountains, and small creatures ran among the bushes. How they maintained such a verdant landscape in a land of bitter cold winters was a closely guarded secret known only to the royal family. The mystery was passed down from queen to princess, but only when the princess reached the age of one hundred. It was knowledge that Galessel had looked forward to inheriting someday. Now, with her status in question, she wondered if she would.

"Well?" Galessel prompted her mother as they walked along the path.

"You know as well as I do that we could meet her demands for increased shipments of coffee, but I'm reluctant to agree. Queen Victoria would have a monopoly on our exports if she could, and resell our beans at exorbitant prices back to those who would have no other option but to buy from Ashelon."

"Mother, it's time to stop avoiding the topics we both know must be talked about."

Her mother stopped briefly to admire a rare black lily at the edge of the path.

"I know you're concerned about the well-being of the fae in Arturia, Daughter. But you know as well as I that matters became more complicated after what befell you."

Though frustrated with the reply, Galessel took her mother's offered hand as they resumed their walk. She'd always found comfort in her mother's touch. "More complicated how? The involvement of the Svellvega with the Ashelon crown doesn't change the plight of our people. It makes it worse."

"Exactly. If it was only that, we might be able to do something. But when they attacked you, they declared war on the Hidden Lands. We must focus on our own lands now."

Galessel stopped, letting go of her mother's hand. She knew she shouldn't be surprised at her mother's isolationist views, but she hadn't seen how the poor and the fae were treated in Arturia. "Ashelon is turning to the Svellvega for aid and likely troops. Stopping Victoria will impede the Svellvega and aid our people."

"That's a valid idea," Galessel's father said as he appeared from behind them on the garden path. Her mother started; it was an uncharacteristic reaction, and an indication of the strain her mother was under. Taller than his wife by more than a hand's breadth, the king was still in his prime, muscular and fit, though the stress of ruling the Hidden Lands through the trials of the Great Unveiling had left its mark. There was tightness around King Valandil's eyes and a heaviness of heart one could see in his face.

"Thank you, Father. It's not just our people suffering in Ashelon, but humans, too. Victoria's withholding food and supplies from her people."

"You have proof of this?" Thessalia resumed walking, knowing Galessel and her father would follow her.

Galessel knew that gut feelings and the story of one gnome's plight wouldn't be enough to sway her mother, but she couldn't let the topic drop. "No, nothing tangible. Yet." Her mother gave her that look. The one that said she'd had enough of the discussion. As she often did, Galessel pushed on. "But you didn't see them like I did, Mother. It's dismal, grey, and choking in Arturia. Human and fae alike are packed together like firewood in the cities, looking for work, trying to survive. And Victoria doesn't care."

Valandil put a hand on Galessel's arm. His eyes held the shadows of deep pain as he guided her toward their outdoor dining hall. "Daughter, we feel for the plight of our people in Arturia, but they chose to stay there when the world changed. It is not our place to insist, by force, as I believe you are implying, that Victoria do her duty by her people. We simply don't have the resources to do so." He offered his wife his arm and took Galessel's hand in his. "Come. It's time for a repast. We can discuss what to do about the Svellvega over fruit and chilled Grey Wind wine."

Chapter 10

Galessel walked through the antechamber on her way to see the Queen of Ashelon. Gone for months, she was anxious to get back to her duties as an ambassador for her people. Though she continued to walk, the door to the queen's receiving room came no closer. From the shadows appeared two Svellvega elves; their eyes glowed an eerie ice blue, and malice dripped like sweat from their bodies. Galessel attempted to turn and run, but her feet stuck to the floor, as the elves approached her with sharp-edged blades held at the ready.

Blood dripped off the knife, as it passed before her eyes. Pain lanced through her ears, and cruel laughter echoed off the walls, threatening to drive Galessel mad.

"Wouldn't want these ears to be too pretty for the queen, now would we?" the Svellvega pirate captain sneered.

Galessel screamed and thrashed, trying to escape.

"Galessel," a distant voice called to her from the mist beyond her sight.

"Galessel, wake up!"

She woke to her mother shaking her gently.

"Be still, my daughter, you are safe," her mother told her gently, gathering the sobbing Galessel in her arms. "Shh, child. The rogues who did this to you are dead. There is nothing to fear anymore."

Galessel pushed away from her mother. "How can you say that? The Svellvega still live. My bodyguards, Daylor and Garrik, are dead. How can I ever feel safe again?" Galessel turned from her mother, trying to hide her tears. She clutched her hands to her chest to keep them from her throbbing ears.

Her mother put a gentle hand on her shoulder. "We

will assign you new guards, and your father has increased the guardians on our borders. When you return to Ashelon, the *Intrepid* will have a full squad of our best men on board. Captain N'hena is increasing the airship's armaments, as well. The Svellvega will not attack her so readily again."

"How can you think to send me back to Queen Victoria? She dismissed me from her court, banned all royals as ambassadors." Galessel pointed to her ears and turned back toward her mother. "Not to mention, by all accounts, I should be banished from our realm, from all of the Hidden Lands, and my name wiped from the scrolls of our people!" She began to sob again, harder this time, and her mother pulled her once again into her embrace.

"My daughter, be still. The *Dien-Vek* has not been done to anyone in the realms of the Hidden Lands for more than two centuries, and it was not sanctioned to be performed on you. Word of the attack on the *Intrepid* and you has been spread across our kingdom, and couriers are even now spreading word to the rest of the Hidden Lands. You will not be shunned for what was done to you. Those same couriers carry an invitation to the rulers of the realms. In a few weeks' time, we will hold the *Fallana Sian*—"

At the mention of the forgiveness ceremony, Galessel again pushed away from her mother. "Why do I need to be forgiven? This was done *to me*! I did not ask for this!" she raged, getting out of bed to pace before the mirror. Before her mother could stop her, she ripped the bandages from her ears, exposing the red and ragged edges. "The Svellvega did this to me!" she screamed, as her mother approached with her hands held out in apology.

Her mother blanched at the sight of her daughter's mutilated ears, but continued to her side. "Galessel, my daughter, of course this is not your fault. The Svellvega will pay for what they have done. Your father and I have both sworn it. The *Fallana Sian* is not to absolve you of any crime, but to show the Hidden Lands that what the Svellvega have done, we will undo."

"But you can't undo this," Galessel sobbed into her mother's shoulder. "The healers can't re-grow my ear tips, and the comet destroyed our glamour. I cannot hide what has been done to me. The magic from the comet was a divine curse. Even our most powerful mages and witches cannot break it, and they've been trying for the last fifty years. I'm doomed to look like this forever."

Thessalia guided her daughter back to sit on the bed. "Dear one, there are other ways to restore what has been taken." She raised Galessel's chin to look her in the eye. "Trust me? Though I cannot give you your ears back as they were, the *Fallana Sian* is also a restoration ceremony. I will see my daughter's dignity and self-worth returned. It is not our ears that make us elven, child, but our character and strength of will."

Galessel looked at her mother, but did not ask the question on her tongue. She knew by her mother's tone that she would say nothing more on the subject.

"Now, return to bed, and I will sing to keep the nightmares at bay."

As her mother tucked her back into bed, Galessel couldn't help but feel like a young child again, frightened by a dream of orcs. She wondered what her mother had planned for the *Fallana Sian*. It had only been performed once in the history of her people. She'd heard the story so often as a child, she could recite it by rote.

Her grandmother's voice filled her mind. "More

than two hundred years ago, when I was just a girl, the elven witch Ravae summoned demons to help defend the Hidden Lands against a vampire horde. They were a nasty lot, but the demons were nastier and dispatched them without much effort. Summoning demons was not Ravae's best decision in hindsight, but it wasn't a crime." Her grandmother would always wink at her then. "It was the 'fact' that she let them loose afterward to ravage a small village of gnomes, that was her crime. Ravae was found guilty of letting the demons loose, and her ears were docked in a ceremony called the *Dien-Vek*. To add insult to injury, she was banished." Her grandmother would always pause for effect, then tweak her nose affectionately. "But fear not, dear one, not long after her banishment, it was discovered that Ravae had been set up. The 'demons' who attacked the village were actually a warrior caste of dryads in war paint who had a grudge against both Ravae and the village, and the 'witnesses' presented at the trial had been under a spell," her grandmother would say in an exasperated tone. "To make amends for the wrong done to Ravae, the queen created the *Fallana Sian* ceremony. Afterward, Ravae was welcomed back into the Hidden Lands with open arms and treated like the hero she was."

Galessel always clapped at the end of the story, happy that Ravae, a hero to her people, had won in the end. Galessel didn't feel like a hero, but she desperately wanted the approval of her people. Her thoughts became muddy as she drifted off to sleep. Her mother's soft, clear voice filled her room, singing of sun-dappled forests and playful fauns and satyrs.

Chapter 11

Staring in the mirror, Galessel contemplated her red, mutilated ears. The face that peered back at her still had its elven features: the high cheekbones, the slightly up-tilted and dappled eyes, but nothing peeked through her hair anymore. Slamming her hairbrush down on the polished marble of her boudoir table, she turned from the mirror in disgust.

Galessel tried to keep the tears at bay, but couldn't. Though the *Dien-Vek* was not done to her as a legal punishment, the ramifications of the act were still life-altering. Even with the upcoming *Fallana Sian*, there would be those who would see her as something less. Her voice wouldn't carry as much weight anymore. The humiliation of being dismissed from Victoria's court was nothing compared to the loss of her ear tips and charms. The visual markers of who she was, what she'd done, were gone. There wasn't enough soft flesh on her ears to replace them.

A knock on her bedchamber door snapped her out of her thoughts. "Enter," she said, as she hurriedly wiped her eyes.

A blond head topped with ram horns peeked around the door. "Galey?" the lithe faun inquired and entered. The faun, as always, was a riot of color and patchwork, in greens, blues, and a garishly contrasting salmon pink. Galessel jumped up from her chair and rushed to embrace her childhood friend.

"Clove! Oh how I have missed you so. When did you return?" Galessel asked, holding her friend in a tight hug.

"Ugh, Galey—you're squeezing me too tight. Let me breathe and I will tell you!"

Galessel let the faun go and stepped back, turning to try to hide her ears from her friend. "Forgive me, Clove.

I'm just so happy to see you. I've been stuck here for what seems like ages, and after what happened—"

Clove took Galessel's shoulders and turned her back around. "I'm sorry, Galey. I came back as soon as I heard, but your mother sent me off again with a message to the centaurs about the *Fallana Sian.* She wouldn't let me stay long enough to see you. I just got back. I haven't even seen your mother yet."

As Clove turned her from side to side to see the damage done to her ears, Galessel lamented, "Oh Clove, what am I to do?" Galessel lowered her head so that her hair fell forward, covering her disfigurement.

Clove guided Galessel to her bed, and they both sat on the edge. "I would kill those pirates myself for what they did to you if N'hena and her crew hadn't done the job already."

The vehemence in Clove's voice helped to dry Galessel's threatening tears and lent her strength. "The captain still lives."

"He does? Argh! If only I could get my hands on him. I'd dock his ears before I ran him through!" Clove got up from the bed and pantomimed a short sword fight, her small steel hooves ringing on the stone tiles. She ended the mock fight with a lunge to her invisible opponent's heart.

Galessel couldn't stop herself from smiling at her friend's antics. Clove seemed to sense the effect on her, and turning with a smile, returned to Galessel's side. "There's my Galey's smile," she said before turning serious again. "You'll get your revenge, Galessel. I swear it. I'll help in any way I can."

"How am I to do that, Clove? I'm banned from the Ashelonian court, and Victoria thinks I'm the one using the silver tongue against her, thanks to that Svellvega scum who is actually manipulating her. Even if I could get another audience, she'd never believe me. And I have no fighting skills to go after the pirate captain, not that Mother or Father would let me join a fighting squad anyway. What kind of revenge can I get?"

Sighing, Clove replied, "I don't know. Yet. But I know between us, we'll think of something. We always do."

She and Clove had become fast friends upon their chance meeting during one of her family's tours through the Wild Lands. They often sought each other out after that, devising ways to sneak away and play and get into trouble. The blame fell equally on them both, though Galessel was usually the one who managed to talk their way out of any punishment.

Clove eventually came to live with the Anisbarii as a fosterling, and she and Galessel became inseparable. As the girls grew into maturity, Galessel was often busy with learning statecraft, and Clove enlisted as the royal family's personal courier, but even with months spent apart, their friendship remained strong.

Shortly after the Great Unveiling, a party of human hunters came upon Clove and her family having a picnic in a meadow. Out of pure malice, they shattered Clove's ankles and slaughtered her husband and young child. Saved by a squad of elven soldiers, Clove was brought back to the Anisbarii to recover.

Galessel stayed by Clove's side for the nearly two years it took her to recover from the painful melding of bone and metal for her new feet, and the enormous effort of learning to walk again. Even with prosthetics designed by the finest gnome craftsmen, it took Clove a long time to adjust to a new way of walking. Distraught and inconsolable for much of that time, it was Galessel's tireless devotion that eventually brought Clove out of her depression.

Clove, in her own way, reminded Galessel that her ruined ears should not define her. If the Svellvega could bring her down so easily, then they'd won. She vowed to show the world that she was made of sterner stuff.

Clove brought Galessel out of her reverie with a tight embrace. "Come on, Galey, cheer up. The Hidden Lands is outraged over what happened to you. You won't be considered an outcast, and after the *Fallana Sian*, no one will dare treat you as one, even if they wanted to."

"The damned Svellvega. I wish we could just wipe them off the map!" Galessel stood and paced. "I know why Mother and Father won't move against them immediately. Our forces aren't ready. We've been at peace for too long. And they claim to have the backing of Asher, but dear Mother Goddess, they've been a scourge on the Hidden Lands for centuries now!"

Clove approached Galessel and stopped her friend's pacing with a gentle hand on her arm. "Galessel, you know as well as I that Asher is nothing to scoff at. He's the god of chaos and strife. He sent the comet as his harbinger, and he turned the human queen into what amounts to his high priestess. I know you want revenge for what the Svellvega did to you, and you'll get it. But I know you don't want it at the expense of your own people."

Galessel sank onto a nearby chair, defeated. "No, I would not willingly sacrifice anyone for my personal desires." She looked up at Clove, her eyes pleading. "We've declared war against the Svellvega, and there is a chance Asher could pull Queen Victoria and her armies into the conflict just for his own amusement. The Hidden Lands and its peoples could be destroyed. I don't want that to happen, but I don't know what to do." Her hand strayed to her ear, recoiling at the unfamiliar feel of its edge. She tucked her hand under her thigh and tried to hold back tears.

Clove looked down at Galessel, unable to hide the pity in her eyes. "What you'll do is be the princess everyone knows you to be. The *Fallana Sian* is in two days' time. I know the ceremony will be hard, but I'll be right there with you, along with your family. And after that, well, I'm not sure what we'll do. But we'll figure it out. Maybe you can go back to Ashelon as an adviser to your replacement."

Though Galessel did not smile, her mood lightened. Something Clove said sparked an idea. "You are right, my dear friend. Getting back to Ashelon is exactly what I need to do."

Chapter 12

Galessel heard Clove's hooves clicking on the stone floor before her friend knocked on the door. "Come!" she said at the same time Clove knocked. "I didn't think you'd still be up."

"I couldn't sleep. Something's felt wrong all evening," Galessel replied, turning from her writing desk to face her friend. Clove's ears drooped, and Galessel swore she looked pale, though it would be impossible to tell through the fine fur covering her face. She got up and went to her friend, leading Clove to a small couch set near the doors that opened on to her private patio. "What's happened?"

The stomp of several pairs of boots in the hall reached her ears. "What's going on, Clove?"

"An airship transporting delegates from the ogre, goblin, and bean-sidhe clans was shot down earlier this evening by the Svellvega. Word just reached us." Clove looked at her hands, shaking on her knees. "There were no survivors."

Galessel's heart stopped, then resumed, beating quickly. "Gentle Goddess, no."

Another knock at her door, this time louder, made both her and Clove jump. Galessel could guess who was at the door. She gripped Clove's hand tightly, then released it, standing and walking to her wardrobe to get a shawl. "Come," she said as she wrapped her favorite blue woven aranak shawl around her shoulders. She faced the door standing tall.

Her mother and father entered, leaving a squad of guards behind them. Dressed in full armor, the guards lined the hall with their swords drawn. Light from the sunstone lamps glinted off helm and greave, nearly blinding Galessel. Her father nodded at Clove and closed the door behind him. The lines around his eyes were deeper. "Somehow I knew you would get here first to break the news, Clove."

Clove shrugged her shoulders, knowing the statement was simply that, and not a rebuke.

"How many were killed?" Galessel asked. She knew her mother would skate around the hard facts if she let her.

"Twenty-five in the ambassadors' parties, plus the thirty crew of the *Beatle*," her father answered.

Her mother's eyes were red from crying, though no tears were evident now. "Those who saw the attack said the *Beatle* never saw their attackers until it was too late. The Svellvega ship came out of a bank of clouds. They gave no quarter." Thessalia paused for a moment, holding back tears. "The poor souls that survived the crash had their throats slit by a Svellvega landing party."

Galessel sank slowly to the floor, unable to comprehend what her mother had just said.

"And I'm afraid there's more," her father said, his voice barely above a whisper. "Many of our messengers have not returned, and hawks carrying word of the attack on you and of the *Fallana Sian* are overdue at the aerie."

Galessel was still putting all the pieces together in her head when Clove's quiet voice broke the silence. "So either the Svellvega anticipated the *Fallana Sian* or there is a spy within the palace?"

King Valandil nodded. "We know not which, thus the guards outside." He looked down at Galessel, his face a mask of sadness, but rage burned in his eyes. "I'm sorry, my daughter, but we cannot hold the ceremony now. We cannot vouch for the safety of the dignitaries who would attend. At least, not until we've found the source of this evil."

The heat that had slowly been building in Galessel's stomach since Clove broke the news began to infuse her entire body. All of the rage she'd kept bottled up threatened to explode. But she held it in check. Her family was not its target. She stood, her fingernails digging into the palms of her hands. "I know the source of this evil. It is the Svellvega, and the head of the snake sits at Victoria's right hand! We should confront her now and remove this plague before it can take hold."

Galessel's mother sighed. "We cannot act rashly, daughter. Storming into Arturia and accusing Victoria of breaking our treaty would only make things worse."

Galessel opened her mouth to protest, but her mother's upheld hand stilled her voice.

"We know what you saw in Victoria's receiving room, Galessel. But right now it is your word against hers, and she will not hesitate to reveal your gift and use it against you." Thessalia shook her head. "Would that you had shown more restraint in Ashelon. Now that the Svellvega know of your silver tongue, they will use it to cast doubt and mistrust among those who would see the Hidden Lands diminished."

Her mother's words stung, rendering her speechless for a moment. She knew the ramifications of using her gift. But what good was it if she couldn't use it—especially in the service of her people? "I wouldn't undo my actions even if I could," Galessel said, tired of always having to justify herself. "If I hadn't used my gift, we wouldn't know about the Svellvega's ties to Victoria. At least now we can prepare for Victoria's betrayal."

Galessel's mother opened her mouth to reply, her eyes angry, but she was cut off by Valandil. "Just so, but your mother is right. If you hadn't used your gift, the Svellvega likely wouldn't have been called in to protect the queen from you, and the discussion would have surely been less heated. Your gift has its price, and I fear this time, while indirectly, it cost people their lives." He came to Galessel, placing his hands on her shoulders. He looked down on her, his countenance sad. "I know you want to help, daughter, but in light of the attacks, I cannot let you leave the palace."

Was she being punished now? The edict made no

sense and she said so. "I don't understand, Father. I can still fulfill my duties as ambassador to the beings of the Hidden Lands. Now more than ever you need me out there, talking to our allies."

Valandil sighed, and her mother refused to meet her eyes when Galessel looked to her.

"I'm sorry, Galessel. After what has happened, without the *Fallana Sian*, our allies will look on you as an outcast, a criminal." He squeezed her hands to forestall her protest. "Hear me out, Daughter. We cannot risk sending you outside the palace. Those that know the truth of what happened to you are few, and while we will send word again, there's no guarantee that those messengers will get through before you would arrive." When shame made her look away, Valandil turned her face back to his with a gentle hand. "Do not be ashamed, Galessel. We will rectify this, but we need time. We need to push the Svellvega back to their ice-forsaken land. Once that's done, we can hold the *Fallana Sian*, and all will be right again."

Galessel pushed away from her father and turned from him, hugging her arms around herself. Punishment or not, she was still a prisoner of fate. How long would it take to rid the air of Svellvega raiders? What if Victoria got involved? What would happen to her people in Ashelon while she withered away in the palace? She flinched when her mother's hand touched her shoulder. Nearly a month after the attack and she still jumped at every little noise and touch. Would it ever stop? Her mother gently turned her around.

"Would it be so awful to spend some time with me in the palace?" Her voice held the slightest trace of hurt. "I would welcome your company while your father is fighting the Svellvega."

Defeated by the look in her mother's eyes, Galessel relented. "No, of course not, Mother. But you know how I dislike being idle."

Her mother laughed. "Well I do. Of my daughters, you always had the most energy. Do not despair. There is plenty you can do to help the Hidden Lands within these walls. You will not waste away."

Thessalia gathered Galessel into an embrace. Over her mother's shoulder, Galessel caught Clove's eye. The faun had been silent through all of this, no doubt taking it all in and deciphering the subtext as well. Clove gave Galessel the barest of nods. They would talk later.

Chapter 13

The shadow of a patrolling airship darkened the path ahead of them for the barest of moments, but its passage left a lingering chill in the air of the warm and inviting palace garden. Normally vibrant tropical blooms seemed to have lost their luster, hiding in the shadows where the glint of sunlight off crystal triggered memories of flashing knife blades. Galessel tried not to shrink in on herself as she walked the winding path with Clove. She very deliberately kept her shoulders back and her head high. Even if she didn't feel strong at the moment, she vowed that no one would know. But Clove did.

"Galey, we don't have to do this. I will stay with you for as long as this takes," Clove said, her ears drooping slightly, as she tracked the airship through the sky. "You did the same for me when my feet were mutilated."

Galessel shook her head. "No, I need to do this. I can't stay cooped up in the palace like some princess in a human story. Mother doesn't really need me. She's not one to be sentimental or get lonely when Father's away. I can do more good back in Arturia, trying to figure out what exactly Victoria's up to."

Clove's ears perked up, swiveling around, searching for signs they weren't alone. When she was satisfied, she drew Galessel over to a stone bench tucked under the branches of a weeping willow. Once they'd both sat, Clove leaned in close and put her hand in front of her mouth. "If you're truly serious about returning to Ashelon to help our people, then there is something you should know," Clove whispered.

Galessel felt like she and Clove were back to being wayward children, plotting how to annoy the troll under the palace bridge. She held back a giggle at the thought. "Why all the secrecy, Clove?" Galessel whispered back.

Clove's ears turned back in annoyance. "This isn't a

childhood plot, Galey. You're talking about going against your parents' wishes and possibly committing treason to help your fellow fae, and even worse to some, humans."

Treason? Was that what she was about to do? Was helping others really that large of an offense? Getting revenge on the Svellvega who mutilated her certainly wasn't. "I've already had my ears docked, Clove, and I'm leaving my home as an unofficial exile. What's worse than that?"

"You could lose your life, Galessel." Clove looked at her for a long moment before continuing. Galessel got the distinct impression she was being evaluated. "To avoid getting caught, you won't be able to stay at the townhouse or circulate among the nobles as you're used to. Your privilege will be gone. You'll have to hide your ears, even hide your race at times. I have connections, but even they may balk at a doubly-exiled princess."

Galessel opened her mouth to refute Clove's last claim, but closed it again, knowing her friend was right.

Clove's eyes softened, and she took Galessel's hands in her own. "What we're about to do is going to be the hardest thing you've ever done. But it also could be the most worthwhile."

Fear warred with resolve. Galessel had been in dangerous situations before, but she'd always had bodyguards and retainers at her back. If she did this, it was just her and Clove, and whoever these contacts of hers were. Galessel had always been more self-reliant than her sisters, but this, this was beyond anything she'd ever done. It wasn't too late to change her mind. There was still a lot of good she could do, even if it was just writing and responding to letters from the other fae factions. She could probably find ways to sneak supplies to her people in Ashelon. Everyone else would be focused on the war with the Svellvega. And she would be safe.

Clove watched her, with one ear constantly swiveling, as she sat there, deciding on which path to take. She squeezed her friend's hands once and stood, squaring her shoulders. As she'd said before, she would not cower behind palace walls. It was exactly what Victoria and the Svellvega expected her to do. It was time for her to truly grow up and take her place in the world, even if, right now, she wasn't sure what that was.

"Meet me by the western stables an hour after midnight. We're going back to Arturia."

Clove smiled, giving Galessel a deep bow before saying, "As you will, Your Highness." With a click of her feet on the cobbles, she bounded away to prepare. As she disappeared around a corner, Galessel heard her giggle. She smiled and headed back to her rooms.

TO BE CONTINUED…

About the Author

Carolyn Kay is a scientist by day, and an author, dancer, knitter, and herbalist by night. She's attempting to raise two fine felines with the help of her husband, Chaz Kemp. (The results are mixed. *Looking at you, Sif*) She also occasionally channels a fae changling, named Cinder. You can catch up on her latest shenanigans at carolynkayauthor.com, or on Twitter @bewitchinghips.

About the Artist

Chaz Kemp is the self-described Art Monkey Supreme behind all of the fabulous art of Ashelon. His origins are clouded in fantastical mystery. Was he found under a rock as his mother claims, or is he really a fae son of the King of the Faeries? We may never know. What we do know is that Chaz is an accomplished artist, musician, actor, and fur-kid father. You can find him at ChazKemp.com and support his work at Patreon.com\chazkemp.